Because Love Alone Wasn't Enough

SARIKA SAREEN

BLUEROSE PUBLISHERS
India | U.K.

Copyright © Sarika Sareen 2025

All rights reserved by author. No part of this publication may be reproduced, stored in a retrieval system or transmitted in any form or by any means, electronic, mechanical, photocopying, recording or otherwise, without the prior permission of the author. Although every precaution has been taken to verify the accuracy of the information contained herein, the publisher assume no responsibility for any errors or omissions. No liability is assumed for damages that may result from the use of information contained within.

BlueRose Publishers takes no responsibility for any damages, losses, or liabilities that may arise from the use or misuse of the information, products, or services provided in this publication.

For permissions requests or inquiries regarding this publication, please contact:

BLUEROSE PUBLISHERS
www.BlueRoseONE.com
info@bluerosepublishers.com
+91 8882 898 898
+4407342408967

ISBN: 978-93-7139-419-2

Cover design: Daksh
Typesetting: Tanya Raj Upadhyay

First Edition: May 2025

Gratitude

First and foremost, I bow my head in deep gratitude to the Supreme Power—for being my guiding light through every moment of doubt, every pause between words, and every spark of inspiration. Without divine grace, this journey would never have begun.

To my father, your unwavering love, guidance, and belief in me have been my foundation.

To my friend Raman, thank you for your boundless encouragement and for being the light that kept my spirit lifted.

To my readers, thank you for embracing this story. If it touches even one heart, it will have all been worth it.

To the team of Blue Rose Publications for your support and hard work. This book wouldn't have been possible without you."

And finally, to the journey itself—thank you for the lessons, the challenges, and the moments of clarity that brought this book to life.

Table of Contents

Chapter 1
Tied by Fate, Touched by Soul.................................... 1

Chapter 2
Step Closer.. 9

Chapter 3
The Burried Emotions.. 16

Chapter 4
A Quiet Escape 24

Chapter 5
Silent Plan of Destiny.. 31

Chapter 6
Echoes of Silence 37

Chapter 7
The Goodbye That Broke Everything....................... 43

Chapter 8
Where Dreams Begin Again 49

Chapter 9
A Heart That Never Moved On 54

Chapter 10
Stillness Between Heartbeats 59

Chapter 11
Silent Threads... 65

Chapter 12
New Beginnings: A Reunion of Hearts 70

Chapter 13
Too Close, Yet Too Far 76

Chapter 14
Silent Words, Heavy Hearts............................. 82

Chapter 15
The Night I Couldn't Pretend 88

Chapter 16
The Silence That Said It All 94

Chapter 17
Between the Pages of Our Love 100

Chapter 18
The Echo Between Doubts and Desires....................... 106

Chapter 19
Entangled in Desire 112

Chapter 20
A Love That Felt Like Home 118

Chapter 21
Living in the Bubble................................. 125

Chapter 22
The Crossroads of the Heart 133

Chapter 23
When Love is Not Enough............................. 139

Chapter 24
Not Every Love Gets a Forever 144

Epilogue 150

Behind the Scenes: From My Heart to Yours 153

Chapter 1

Tied by Fate, Touched by Soul

The night crackled with energy.

Fairy lights draped across rooftops, casting a golden glow on everything beneath.

Music pulsed like a heartbeat, drawing students into its rhythm.

The college fest was in full swing—wild, carefree, and alive with endless possibility. On the edge of it all stood Ajay.

Ajay

He was quiet yet confident, an introvert who spoke more through his presence than his words. Tall and lean, with sharp features and a steady gaze, he carried an effortless charm that didn't seek attention but somehow always drew it. His calm aura and deep, observant eyes gave him a quiet magnetism, drawing attention even when he wished to remain unseen.

Dressed in a simple lime green kurta and dark blue jeans, Ajay faded into the crowd. His gaze wandered aimlessly, his mind lost in distant "what ifs" and "maybes," untouched by the celebration around him. In the final year of his computer engineering degree, he stood quietly at the crossroads of dreams and doubts.

The evening sky glowed orange and pink above, but his focus was inward—until she appeared.

Sana

Sana entered like a burst of energy — loud, confident, and full of life, as though she was meant to fill every corner of the room with her spirit. Her laughter rang out, uncontained and joyful, like music that couldn't be ignored. Her long, straight hair framed her face, catching the light as she moved, while her fair skin glowed with a natural radiance. Dressed in a hand-painted floral suit, she didn't need to try to stand out; she simply did. There was a freedom in the way she moved, a sense that the world was hers to explore, filled with endless adventures.

In her final year of college, studying child psychology, Sana was as passionate about understanding people as she was about living her own life to the fullest. Her love for travel, her deep connection with happiness, and her dreams that reached far beyond what others expected — all of it made her unshakable. Tonight, she was here to enjoy the moment, laughing with her cousin Anaya, ready to make new memories with her heart wide open.

Anaya and Ajay had been in the same year and class throughout college. While Ajay remained a quiet, reserved presence, Anaya often turned to him for help with notes. His thorough explanations and patient nature made him an unlikely but dependable academic ally. They never exchanged much more than a few words during those sessions, but there was an unspoken understanding between them.

"Ajay, meet my cousin Sana," Anaya said, pulling him from his thoughts.

Ajay turned—and there she was. Her eyes locked onto his with a glint of mischief and curiosity, as though she had just stepped out of a dream, he hadn't realized he was waiting for.

"Nice to meet you," she said, extending her hand, her smile effortless and bold.

Ajay hesitated for a beat, momentarily taken aback by her energy. Then, as if something quietly shifted, he reached out. "Nice to meet you," he replied, his voice quieter, but steady. A strange flutter stirred in his chest—familiar, yet foreign.

There was something in the air between them. Something unsaid.

They came from different worlds—Ajay, with his calm intellect and introverted charm, and Sana, with her fearless curiosity and radiant spirit. But something about their encounter lingered.

As the night unfolded, Ajay caught himself watching her. She moved like music—fluid, vibrant. Her laughter was infectious, her conversations sharp yet light. Though she was young, there was a quiet depth in her, a grounded confidence that surprised him.

Their paths crossed again when Anaya insisted Ajay join them at the food stalls.

"Come on, Ajay, stop being such a loner! One night with us won't hurt," she said, giving him a playful shove.

Before he could answer, Sana jumped in, her voice teasing. "Or maybe he's just holding out for better company?"

Their eyes met, and for a second, the world shrank around them.

"I think I can make some time," Ajay said, trying to sound casual, though her words had left an impact.

As they walked, the conversation naturally shifted to future plans.

They took a corner table near the food stalls, a little away from the crowd, where it was actually possible to talk and hear each other. The fairy lights overhead cast a soft glow, and the distant music now felt like a gentle hum in the background.

Sana stirred her cold coffee, leaning slightly forward. "So... what about you, Ajay? I've been doing all the talking. What are *your* dreams?"

Ajay looked at her, thoughtful. "Dreams, huh?" He paused, as if weighing his words. "I guess... I've always wanted to travel. Click pictures of places no one notices. Corners of the world that aren't loud but still have stories."

"That's beautiful," Sana said quietly. "You seem like someone who finds meaning in the little things."

"I try," he replied with a shy smile. "It's easy to miss the little things when you're caught up in trying to prove yourself all the time."

She looked at him, sensing there was more behind that sentence. "Tough expectations at home?"

Ajay nodded. "Yeah. My dad believes in discipline and stability—government job, secure future, no nonsense. I don't blame him. He just wants me to be safe in a world that's constantly shifting."

Sana softened, her voice gentle. "And what do *you* want?"

He glanced at her, surprised by the question. Most people never asked that.

"I want to build a life that makes sense to *me*. One that lets me breathe," he said finally.

What about you, Sana?

I aspire to specialize in child psychology, driven by a deep passion for helping children navigate their emotional challenges. I wish to open my own clinic, a safe haven where young minds could find understanding and support. Its my vision to work closely with children struggling with anxiety, behavioral issues, or the weight of societal and familial expectations, providing them with the tools to heal and thrive. This dream isn't just a career goal for me; it is a heartfelt mission to make a difference in their lives, one step at a time.

"That's... amazing, Sana," Ajay said, his voice soft but filled with admiration. "Not many people think about things like this, let alone dedicate their lives to it. You have such a kind heart."

Sana held his gaze, her smile touched with surprise and sincerity. "Thank you, Ajay. That means more than you know."

The conversation flowed easily from there. Sana asked him about his studies, and Ajay opened up about his love for coding and his growing interest in photography. She listened closely, her questions thoughtful and curious—even when the topics were unfamiliar to her.

They couldn't ignore how different they were—not just in personality, but in upbringing. Ajay came from a conservative family, where discipline and restraint were valued. His father, a stern man with little tolerance for distractions, had always insisted that Ajay focus on academics and stability. Their lifestyle was simple, grounded in tradition and hard work.

In contrast, Sana came from a wealthy and open-minded Punjabi family. Her world was vibrant, full of color, freedom, and loud opinions. She carried herself with grace and confidence, unafraid to speak her mind or chase her passions.

Their worlds couldn't have been more different—Ajay's rooted in quiet structure, and Sana's blooming with bold energy. Yet, despite these contrasts, something about their presence together felt easy.

Perhaps it was Sana's playful spirit or Ajay's steady calm. But their differences didn't feel like barriers—they felt like pieces of a puzzle slowly coming together.

For Ajay, it was rare to feel seen. Yet with Sana, her interest didn't feel forced. She genuinely wanted to know him.

As the evening wore on, they found themselves strolling back toward the main campus. "I didn't expect to enjoy this as much as I did," Ajay confessed quietly, his eyes on the path ahead.

Sana smiled, walking beside him. "It's not about the fest, is it? It's about the people."

He stopped for a second, her words settling deep. She was right. The fest wasn't what made this night special—it was her.

"Well, I'm glad we met," he said, his voice softer now, more personal. "Maybe we'll bump into each other again?"

Sana's eyes sparkled with that familiar mischief. "Oh, I'm sure we will. The universe has a funny way of crossing paths again."

As they parted ways that night, both Ajay and Sana couldn't shake the feeling that this was the beginning of something. They didn't know what it was, or where it would lead, but the anticipation hung in the air like the final notes of a beautiful song yet to be fully played.

For now, all they knew was that they wanted to see each other again, and perhaps, the next meeting would reveal a little more of what their connection truly meant.

"Some connections feel timeless, as if souls know each other before the mind does."

Chapter 2

A Step Closer...

There was something about their connection that felt different—like an old soul bond pulling them together. Ajay couldn't understand why he was feeling this way. He, who always buried himself in assignments and studies, now found himself waiting for a message or a call from her. He had never felt attracted to any girl like this before. What was it about her that had made him feel so distracted? What charm had she cast on him? He couldn't explain it, but he couldn't stop thinking about her.

The next week felt like a dream, as if everything was falling into place. Each day felt like it was filled with a quiet tension, as if something more was just around the corner. Time seemed to slow down, teasing them both with the feeling that something was about to happen. The sun rose and set, bringing hope, while the moon brought quiet thoughts of longing. Ajay, more distracted than ever, found his mind drifting to Sana whenever he had a moment. His heart would skip a beat whenever his phone buzzed, only to feel disappointed when it wasn't her.

Sana, too, felt the excitement building. She thought about their conversations again and again, wondering what could happen next. The sound of her laughter seemed to linger in the air, as if the breeze itself was carrying her smile to him. Everything around them felt like it was pushing them closer, day by day. It was as though something deeper was pulling them together, though neither of them could quite explain it yet.

Anaya, with her natural intuition, could effortlessly sense the unspoken emotions that lingered between Ajay and Sana. Though their story seemed destined from the start, she became the quiet force that gently brought them together, a silent bridge connecting their hearts. It was as if fate had chosen her as the thread that would bind their lives, weaving together the delicate strands of their unexpressed feelings.

Anaya finally decided to step in, sensing that the time had come to unite these two souls whose fates seemed inseparably intertwined. With a heart brimming with hope and a glimmer of hint of mischief, she crafted a plan to bring them face-to-face. She knew that the feelings brewing between them were deep, yet veiled by hesitation and unspoken words.

Ajay, with his quiet shyness and guarded heart, would never take the first step. He was too reserved, his emotions hidden like secrets behind his steady gaze. But Anaya believed that once their paths crossed closely enough, the invisible pull between them would leave no room for restraint. So, she planned the perfect setting for their meeting.

So, she picked the perfect place for them to meet—a cozy bookshop nearby, filled with the smell of old books and fresh coffee. The soft lighting and quiet atmosphere made it the kind of place where people could get lost in their thoughts.

Sana, who loved books, felt right at home here. Ananya had invited Ajay for a casual visit, telling him she need to study some of his notes, and brought Sana along with her. The bookshop was calm and peaceful, making it the perfect place for something special to happen.

As they wandered through the aisles, their eyes met. There was something in the way Ajay looked at Sana that made his heart race. Her gaze was warm and inviting, and for a moment, it felt like the world around them disappeared. The quiet of the bookstore seemed to make everything feel more intense, drawing them closer without either of them saying a word.

Sana's heart skipped a beat, realizing that this was the moment she had secretly been waiting for. Surrounded by books she loved, the calmness of the store, and Ajay's presence, it felt like everything was falling into place.

As they found themselves standing just a heartbeat away from each other, there was a softness in the air, a kind of magic that wrapped around them like a warm embrace.

Ananya, sensing the right moment, decided to step away, leaving Ajay and Sana alone in the quiet comfort of the bookstore. She gave them both a knowing smile before disappearing.

After a few moments, Ajay cleared his throat, his voice hesitant but soft. "Would you like to go for some ice cream?" he asked, his lips curving into a shy smile. Sana's face lit up, her eyes sparkling with excitement as she nodded.

The warm afternoon carried a gentle breeze as they walked side by side toward the ice cream parlor. The scent of blooming flowers mingled with the summer air, and Sana's laughter rang out softly, lightening Ajay's heart. She had chosen this place—her favorite retreat on days like these. Inside, they found a cozy corner table, bathed in sunlight streaming through the glass doors. The golden rays kissed her skin, illuminating her features, and Ajay couldn't help but marvel at how effortlessly beautiful she looked.

As she savored her hot chocolate with brownie and vanilla ice cream, Sana leaned forward, her gaze steady yet warm. "I don't understand what it is," she began softly, her voice laced with curiosity and something deeper. "This magnetic pull between us—it feels like more than chance. Almost like... some connection from another time, another life. I've never felt this close to anyone before."

Her words hung in the air, resonating in Ajay's chest. He searched her eyes, their depth stirring something in him that he couldn't quite put into words. Ajay wanted to speak, to say what was in his heart, but his thoughts tangled with uncertainty. Instead, he smiled faintly and nodded, letting her words fill the silence between them.

They began to talk, delving into each other's worlds. Sana spoke with enthusiasm, her eyes lighting up as she shared stories of her family, her dreams, and the future she envisioned. She asked Ajay about his own hopes and listened with unwavering interest, her presence like a soothing balm to his otherwise cautious heart.

Ajay, however, found himself holding back. While Sana's confidence and openness drew him in, his mind kept circling back to the invisible barriers that surrounded him. The expectations of his family loomed heavily—Ajay's conservative upbringing and the burden of his modest financial background made the idea of a relationship with someone like Sana feel like an impossible dream. He knew his father, with his strict principles and focus on building a secure future, would never approve of such a match. The fear of disappointing his family and the glaring disparity between their worlds stopped Ajay from thinking too far ahead.

Sana noticed his hesitation but didn't push him. She simply smiled and let him take his time. Her warmth and understanding were enough to show him that she cared.

As the afternoon passed, a quiet connection grew between them. The sunlit room, the sweetness of shared ice cream, and the unspoken feelings created a bond that words couldn't explain. Even without saying it aloud, they both knew this wasn't just any ordinary meeting. It felt like the start of something timeless.

When it was time to part, the moment grew heavy with unspoken words and lingering emotions. Neither of them wanted to leave, but the outside world called them back. As they exchanged numbers, there was a quiet hope in their eyes, a silent promise to meet again soon.

Sana, with her love for journaling, poured her emotions into the pages of her secret diary that night. She wrote about the connection she felt with Ajay, the way he had already carved a space in her heart. Her feelings for him were growing stronger with each passing day, and in her mind, she had already begun dreaming of a future together, a happily ever after that felt almost within reach.

Yet, a part of her couldn't shake the feeling that something was holding Ajay back. While she could sense his feelings for her, there was a hesitation in his actions, a barrier she couldn't quite identify. Was it someone else? Was he carrying the weight of his family's expectations? These unanswered questions began to gnaw at her, and her suspicion grew as days turned into weeks.

Determined to find clarity, Sana resolved to confront Ajay directly. She needed to know where they stood and if the connection, they shared had a chance to blossom into something real. Her heart wavered between hope and fear, but she knew she couldn't let the uncertainty linger any longer.

"He didn't believe in love at first sight—until she walked in and changed everything."

Chapter 3

The Burried Emotions

Their hearts wavered between hope and fear, but they couldn't let the uncertainty linger any longer. As the days passed, life quickly swept them into its busy rhythm. Ajay, consumed by his exam preparations, found little time for anything beyond his studies. His days were long, filled with books and assignments. Sana, too, was tangled in her own workload, balancing deadlines and projects. They would exchange the occasional message or brief chat, but their conversations remained light and casual, neither of them finding the space for something deeper.

After weeks of stressful exams, Ajay finally felt a sense of relief. But even in his calm, his thoughts kept drifting to Sana. He could tell how deeply she cared for him, and he didn't want to keep her in the dark about his feelings. He knew it was time to talk to her and share his heart.

On a quiet Saturday morning, he called Sana, his voice steady but his heart pounding. "Sana, would you like to join me for dinner tonight?" he asked, picking a peaceful, less crowded place where they could talk freely. He wanted to open up to her, and he hoped she would understand the seriousness of what he needed to say.

Sana's heart skipped a beat as she heard his voice. Dinner with Ajay? Could this be the moment she had dreamed of? Her mind raced with excitement. Maybe tonight was the night he would finally tell her how he felt. A rush of emotions flooded her—hope, joy, and the thrilling possibility of love. As the day went on, she couldn't stop thinking about him, her heart filled with anticipation for what was to come.

Ajay texted her the time and venue, planning a simple yet thoughtful dinner with soft music. In a city like Delhi, full of romantic and fancy restaurants, he chose something quiet and unpretentious.

He didn't need luxury or extravagance, just a place where they could talk. It was the perfect setting for him to open up and share what had been holding him back, hoping she would understand his heart.

Sana looked stunning in a long black dress that perfectly outlined her curves. The fabric had a soft shimmer, making her stand out effortlessly. Her black stilettos added to her height, giving her a touch of elegance and grace.

As she walked, the soft click of her heels caught everyone's attention. Her bold red lips and sparkling eyes added to her charm, making it hard for anyone to look away. She carried herself with such confidence and style that the whole room seemed to focus on her. People stopped to stare, conversations faded, and Sana became the center of everyone's attention without even trying.

Ajay was a striking contrast to Sana's dazzling presence. Dressed in a simple black shirt and a pair of well-fitted denims, his style was understated yet effortlessly attractive. His high cheekbones and deep, expressive black eyes held a quiet intensity that made him undeniably handsome. His fair complexion added to his charm, and though his clothes weren't from any luxury brand, he carried himself with a natural confidence that set him apart from the crowd.

There was something captivating about his simplicity—an aura of calm strength that drew people in without him even trying. Ajay didn't need flashy outfits or extravagant accessories; his charm lay in the way he stood tall, composed, and seemingly oblivious to the attention he was garnering. In that moment, his unassuming presence became its own kind of magnetism.

When their eyes met, something unspoken passed between them—a spark of warmth and connection that neither could ignore. Ajay had arrived before Sana and stood up respectfully as she approached.

"You look gorgeous, Sana," he said softly, his eyes lingering on her for a moment longer than usual.

"Thank you, Ajay," she replied with a warm smile. "You look different too... I mean, you look really handsome. I think everyone's looking at us."

Ajay chuckled nervously, his cheeks turning a faint shade of pink. "I hope that's a good thing," he said, meeting her gaze.

They both smiled shyly, their hearts beating a little faster as the space between them seemed to disappear.

Just then, a waiter came over to take their order, breaking the silence between them.

"What will you have, Sana?" Ajay asked nervously, unsure of her preferences.

"I'll have chicken tikka and a beer," Sana replied with a smile.

Ajay froze for a moment, surprised. He hadn't known Sana was a non-vegetarian. Coming from a strictly vegetarian family, this was yet another difference that added to his growing doubts. As he wrestled with his thoughts, Sana's voice brought him back.

"What about you, Ajay? Will you share this with me, or should I order something else for you?" she asked kindly.

He hesitated before saying softly, "No, Sana, I'm a vegetarian."

"Oh, I didn't know. I'm sorry. You can order something else for yourself," she said, her voice warm and understanding.

Ajay nodded and ordered a paneer wrap. The waiter left with a polite smile, and the air between them grew still again.

"So, Ajay, why did you plan this dinner?" Sana asked, her curiosity evident.

Ajay shifted uncomfortably in his seat, his nerves showing. "It's been a while since we met properly. With exams and assignments, we've both been busy... but there's something important I need to talk to you about."

And there was a complete silence between the two, as if the time has paused.

Sana leaned forward, her expression softening. She reached out and placed her hand gently on his, a gesture of comfort and encouragement. "I'm listening," she said, her voice steady but filled with warmth.

Ajay cleared his throat, his heart pounding. "Sana, before we take this relationship any further, there are things we need to talk about. I care about you, and I know we both feel the same way... but we can't ignore the differences between us. Our families are a big part of our lives, and they'll matter in whatever future we try to build together."

Sana's smile faded, replaced by a thoughtful expression. She gazed into his eyes, searching for the hope she desperately wanted to find. Her silence spoke volumes, but the way she held his hand tighter reassured Ajay.

"I know it's not going to be easy," she said softly, her voice laced with a mix of determination and vulnerability. "But I believe in us, Ajay. Do you?"

Her words hung in the air, filled with unspoken emotions, as they both stared into each other's eyes, feeling the weight of the decision they were about to make together.

"What is it, Ajay? You're scaring me now," Sana said softly, her voice tinged with worry.

Ajay hesitated, his eyes avoiding hers. "Sana... I come from a very conservative family. They're not modern like yours. We're deeply religious and strictly vegetarian. They would expect their daughter-in-law to follow the same values. And... the biggest issue is that they don't believe in love marriages. They've always been clear about that."

He paused, struggling with the words. "Even if, by some miracle, they agreed... I'm scared you wouldn't be able to adjust to their way of life. It's so different from what you're used to."

Sana stared at him, her heart sinking. This was the conversation she had feared but hoped would never happen. She had been dreaming of a future with Ajay—something filled with love, joy, and adventure. But now, those dreams seemed to crumble before her eyes. Her mind struggled to process what he was saying, and for a moment, she was completely silent.

Ajay looked at her, his own heart heavy. He knew this wasn't what she wanted to hear, but he felt trapped. Being his parents' only child, he had always been the center of their world. With that love came expectations so heavy they felt like a cage, holding him back from being himself.

"I've always had my own dreams and passions," he admitted, his voice breaking slightly. "But every time I shared with my parents, they would remind me that they knew what was best for me. So, I kept quiet, pushed everything aside, and tried to be the son they wanted me to be."

Sana's eyes filled with tears as she listened. She could feel his pain and the weight he carried, torn between his love for her and his duty to his family. She reached for his hand again, gripping it tightly, as if to say she wasn't ready to let go.

"Ajay," she whispered, her voice trembling, "we'll figure this out. I don't know how, but we will. I care about you too much to give up without trying."Her words brought a flicker of hope to Ajay's troubled heart, but the road ahead felt more uncertain than ever.

"In her laughter, he found a melody; in his silence, she found a home. And somewhere in between, love began to grow."

Chapter 4

A Quiet Escape

Months passed, and Ajay and Sana grew closer with every moment they spent together. From movies and ice cream parlors to long dinners, they craved each other's company. It was as if the world faded when they were together.

Even though the path ahead was cloaked in uncertainty, they couldn't help but drift toward each other—again and again. It felt as though some cosmic force was pulling them closer, something deeper than logic or reason.

Sana began to dream, not just about love but about a forever. In her heart, she started building silent promises. She believed in this connection with all her heart, and so did Ajay — quietly, deeply, completely.

When Ajay told his parents he was going on a college trip with friends, it was a lie. He had secretly planned a weekend getaway to Udaipur for their first anniversary— a city Sana had always dreamed of exploring. The hotel they chose was a heritage haveli, rich with Rajasthani charm and elegance.

After checking into their room that afternoon, both of them felt the exhaustion of travel. Sana sat in silence, a soft shyness in her presence, while Ajay wrestled with words that refused to come. It was their first moment alone, and the air was alive with unspoken emotions and sweet tension.

Sana sat in silence, a soft shyness in her presence, while Ajay wrestled with words that refused to come. It was their first moment alone, and the air was alive with unspoken emotions and sweet tension.

"Ajay," Sana finally whispered, her voice soft yet sure. "We love each other... and it's okay to be close. This won't change what we feel. If anything, it'll only make us stronger."

She looked at him, her eyes reflecting a vulnerability she had never shown before. Her words hung between them, tender and brave, wrapping them in a fragile cocoon of trust.

Ajay reached out, his fingers trembling slightly as they found hers. He paused, searching her eyes as if trying to read the depths of her soul.

"I don't know where this will take us," he murmured, his voice barely above a whisper, "but I want to be here. With you. No matter the uncertainty, no matter what happens next, I want to hold on to us... to this."

For a moment, neither spoke. The silence between them was heavy with meaning — a quiet understanding, a bond forming that neither of them could fully explain but both felt in their hearts.

He moved closer, cupping her face gently in his hands. Their eyes met, and the unspoken love between them said more than words ever could. He leaned in, capturing her lips in a tender yet passionate kiss.

The tension melted away as their kiss grew deeper, filled with the passion they had been holding back. Sana's fingers traced along Ajay's jaw, while his hands slid around her waist, pulling her closer until there was no space left between them. Their hearts raced as their love spilled over, taking them to a place where nothing else mattered.

Ajay's touch was gentle yet full of desire, and Sana responded with the same intensity, their bodies moving together in perfect harmony. Every glance, every caress spoke of the love they had kept inside for so long.

As their emotions settled, they lay wrapped in each other's arms, the warmth of their love surrounding them like a gentle cocoon. Sana rested her head on Ajay's chest, listening to the steady beat of his heart, while his fingers gently played with her hair. The soft sounds of the haveli faded into the background as they held each other, letting the peace of the moment lull them into a deep, contented sleep.

The next morning, Ajay woke up first. He quietly made two cups of strong coffee, the aroma filling the room. Turning back, he saw Sana still asleep, her face serene, a faint smile lingering on her lips. She looked so beautiful, so at peace, that he didn't have the heart to wake her.

Sitting beside her, Ajay sipped his coffee, his thoughts growing heavy. He stared out the window, wondering about their future. *Will we really be able to be together?* The uncertainty loomed over him like a shadow.

As he glanced back at Sana, the weight of his emotions deepened. She had given him so much love and hope, yet the thought of their families and their different worlds left him conflicted. A quiet sadness settled in, and for a moment, he felt powerless against the destiny that awaited them.

While Ajay was lost in his thoughts, Sana stirred awake and gently touched his hand. Startled, Ajay turned to look at her. Her eyes held a quiet promise, brimming with dreams and hope. Without a word, they embraced, letting the silence weave a conversation of its own.

Soon, they were ready to explore the vibrant charm of Udaipur, a city that had long captivated Sana's imagination. Known as the City of Lakes, Udaipur's allure lay in its intricate palaces, colorful bazaars, and serene waters. Sana's enthusiasm was contagious as she darted from one shop to another in the bustling Hathi Pol Bazaar, admiring delicate Rajasthani juttis, hand-painted miniature artworks, and ornate jewelry.

"Ajay, look at this!" she exclaimed, holding up a vibrant Bandhani dupatta. "Isn't it perfect?" Ajay smiled, amused by her childlike glee, and decided to surprise her by buying it when she wasn't looking.

They wandered through the majestic City Palace, marveling at the intricate architecture and breathtaking views of Lake Pichola. Sana couldn't resist snapping a dozen photos, some candid and some where Ajay was coaxed into smiling.

Lunch was an adventure of its own as they sampled Udaipur's famous dal baati churma at a cozy lakeside café. Sana giggled as Ajay struggled to balance the crisp baati, the ghee, and the sweet churma on his plate. "You're hopeless," she teased, wiping a crumb off his chin.

As the sun began to set, they took a boat ride on Lake Pichola, the calm waters reflecting the golden hues of the setting sun. Ajay found himself mesmerized, not by the scenery but by Sana's laughter, her hair catching the soft glow of the evening.

By the time they returned to their hotel, their bags were heavier, their feet sore, and their hearts lighter. "You know," Sana said as she flopped onto the bed, "this city feels like it's telling a story in every corner."

"Maybe it is," Ajay replied, his voice soft. "And maybe we're part of it now."

Sana's eyes sparkled at his words, her dreams weaving seamlessly with the magic of Udaipur.

Both were exhausted, yet their hearts felt full as they lay in each other's arms, drifting into a peaceful sleep. The weight of unspoken words and shared dreams lingered in the air as they held on to the moment.

The next morning came too soon, bringing with it the reality of their departure. As they packed their bags and prepared to check out, an overwhelming thought crossed both their minds—how quickly these days had flown by. It felt like a dream, one they weren't quite ready to wake up from.

The journey back was quiet, their usual chatter replaced by a reflective silence. Ajay's was quiet, his thoughts miles ahead. Sana gazed out of the window, lost in her own whirlwind of emotions. They both knew what lay ahead.

"We need to tell our families," Sana said softly, breaking the silence.

Ajay glanced at her, nodding, though his chest tightened at the thought. "We should. But..." He hesitated, his voice trailing off.

"But what?" Sana asked, sensing his unease.

"I just have this feeling," Ajay admitted. "I don't know how my family will take it. I can't shake the thought that it won't go as smoothly as we hope."

Sana reached over, her hand gently covering his on the gear shift. "We'll face it together. Whatever happens."

Her words were steady, but her heart raced at the thought of her own family's reactions.

"In each other's arms, they were lost in time, suspended in a bubble where only love existed."

Chapter 5

Silent Plan of Destiny

Few months later, the festival of lights illuminated every corner of the city, and Sana decided it was time. She invited Ajay to her home for Diwali lunch, determined to introduce him to her family officially. Her family was modern and open-minded, and over countless dinners, she had dropped hints about Ajay. Yet, as the moment drew closer, her confidence wavered.

Standing in her room, adjusting the dupatta of her vibrant anarkali dress, Sana felt a knot tighten in her stomach. What if they didn't see Ajay the way she did? What if her parents, who always trusted her, questioned this relationship?

When Ajay arrived, his heart beat just as loudly in his chest. He could sense the importance of the day from Sana's nervous smile. "Are you sure about this?" he asked, his voice low as she welcomed him at the door.

Ajay nodded, bracing himself. Together, they stepped into the next chapter of their lives, unsure of what awaited but ready to face it—hand in hand.

Sana's home was a haven of warmth and love, where every corner seemed to tell a story. The walls adorned with vibrant modern art and the carefully curated décor gave the house an air of perfection—just like Sana herself. Her personality, open-minded and magnetic, was clearly a reflection of her parents. From the moment Ajay stepped inside, they welcomed him with a kindness that made him feel instantly at ease.

Yet, even in this comforting atmosphere, Ajay's mind was restless. As he sat in the living room, observing the lively conversations and the effortless flow of affection between family members, a stark contrast played in his thoughts. His own family, bound by traditions and conservative values, was so different from this easy-going, modern household. *How would these two worlds ever come together?* he wondered. *Would they accept each other?*

His face grew serious as his thoughts deepened. Sensing his preoccupation, Sana's father approached him with a warm smile, holding two glasses of red wine.

"Beta don't think too much. Enjoy your drink, if its in your destiny it wil happen no matter what you plan. And for now, just live in the moment. Ajay smiled and accepted the drink. Although his parents didn't approve of it. And after a brief intoduction from Ajay, the lunch was served.

The room filled with the sounds of laughter and casual conversation; the kind that made time slip by unnoticed. Ajay found himself enjoying the lively atmosphere, appreciating the warmth of a family that felt so different from his own.

After a lavish meal followed by a delightful spread of desserts, it was time for Ajay to leave. As he stood at the door, Sana walked him out, her smile filled with reassurance.

"Thank you for today," he said quietly, his heart brimming with gratitude.

"It's just the beginning," she replied, her voice soft yet firm. "Now it's your turn to take the next step."

And now it was Ajay's turn. On a warm Sunday afternoon when everyone was home, Ajay decided to talk about Sana.

Umm... Clearing his throat he said, "Well I need to share something with you all" "I've been seeing a girl lately, Sana. She's just graduated in psychology and is now preparing for her master's."

I like her. I just want you all to meet her once before taking any decision.

For a moment, silence filled the room. Ajay's words seemed to hang in the air, floating somewhere between surprise and disbelief. His mother paused mid-way through peeling peas; her hands stilled. His father looked up from his Sunday newspaper, his expression unreadable. Even his younger sister, who had been scrolling on her phone, looked up, her eyes wide with curiosity.

Ajay felt the tension ripple across the room, but he kept his composure.

"She's smart, kind, and respectful. I've known her for a while now," he added gently, glancing at his parents. "Her name is Sana. I think it's time you meet her."

His mother was the first to react. "Sana?" she repeated, her voice carrying a note of caution. "Where is she from, Ajay?"

"Delhi. Punjabi family," he replied. "She's completed her graduation in psychology, Mom. Very focused, very grounded. She's also really passionate about working with kids. You'd like her—she knows what she wants and stays true to herself."

His father slowly folded his newspaper and placed it on the table, exhaling deeply. "Punjabi?" he asked quietly, not with anger, but with the weight of a thousand unspoken expectations.

Ajay nodded, knowing this was the part they'd struggle with. His family, deeply rooted in conservative traditions, had always expected him to marry someone from within their own community.

"She's a good person, Papa. And I want you to meet her without any judgment. Just once. After that, you can decide whatever you feel is right."

His mother looked thoughtful, clearly conflicted. "Ajay, we've never stopped you from choosing your path. But marriage is a lifetime bond. It's not just about two people—it's about two families, two cultures, two belief systems."

"I know, Ma," he said earnestly. "And that's why I want you to see the person she is. Not just where she's from."

His father stood up, stretching his arms and walking toward the window. For a long time, he stared outside, as if weighing every possible outcome. Finally, he spoke.

"Invite her," he said, not turning around. "Let's meet her first. We'll talk after that."

Ajay's heart swelled with quiet relief. He knew this wasn't approval. Not yet. But it was a door slightly open, a beginning.

That evening, he called Sana.

"They've agreed to meet you," he said, unable to hide the mix of nerves and excitement in his voice.

Sana gasped, her voice bubbling with cautious optimism. "They did? What did they say? Were they okay with everything?"

"Well... not completely. But they're willing to meet you. That's all that matters for now."

There was a pause on the other end. "I'm nervous, Ajay," she admitted. "What if I say something wrong? What if they don't like me?"

"They will," he assured her gently. "Just be yourself. That's all they need to see."

As she lay awake that night, her heart was caught between hope and fear, between love and uncertainty. Would love be enough to overcome the silence of judgment, the weight of expectations? Or would this be another love story lost in time—only to remain a fleeting memory in the bubble they had created?

"Love is not just about certainty, but about taking the leap despite the doubts."

Chapter 6

Echoes of Silence

The next morning, as they sat around the breakfast table, the air felt thick with unspoken words. Ajay's mother, her expression a mix of love and concern, finally broke the silence. "Ajay, you know how we feel about love marriages," she said, her voice soft but firm. His father remained silent, his face unreadable, as always.

Ajay was quiet, his thoughts swirling. After a long pause, his father spoke, his tone steady but edged with experience. "I'm only agreeing to meet them for you," he said, his voice carrying the weight of years. "I'm still old-fashioned, and I believe in marriages within our community. I've seen the world, Ajay, and trust me—such marriages don't work in the long run."

He paused, his gaze softening slightly as he looked at his son. "Still, let them come on Sunday. We'll talk then."

Ajay nodded, knowing that this was just the beginning of the journey ahead.

The next Sunday, Sana paced restlessly across her room, her stomach tight with nerves. She was excited but also worried. *Will they like us? Will they accept me?* These thoughts wouldn't leave her mind. But the biggest question echoed deeper—*Is love enough to live with a family so different from my own?*

She took a deep breath, stood in front of the mirror, and gave herself a small smile. "Let's do this," she whispered.

Before leaving, Sana gathered her family in the living room. "Listen, we need to keep things simple," she said firmly. "They're not like us. No loud jokes, no being too casual. Just stay polite and calm."

Her parents gave her an amused look but nodded, understanding the seriousness in her voice.

Ajay's house stood on a quiet lane, miles apart in spirit from the lively, colorful world Sana belonged to. The small house had plain white walls and a sturdy wooden door, reflecting the family's simple way of life. The garden out front was neat, with trimmed plants that spoke of discipline and order.

As Sana and her family approached, her heart pounded. The closer they got, the more her confidence wavered.

The simplicity of Ajay's home was unfamiliar, and it reminded her just how far apart their worlds truly were.

Inside, the house was modest but clean. Wooden furniture filled the rooms, and a few family photos hung on the walls. A clock ticked softly in the background, adding to the silence. There were no fancy decorations, just a sense of simplicity and structure.

Ajay welcomed them with a smile, though Sana noticed the tension in his eyes. As her family entered, she followed, trying to hide her nerves.

Everyone sat in the living room, the air feeling heavy with formality. Sana's parents greeted Ajay's family warmly but respectfully, just as she had requested. Ajay's mother observed Sana carefully, her eyes calm but serious. His father remained mostly silent observed Sana carefully.

Behind the polite smiles and formal exchanges, an invisible wall stood tall—made of unspoken judgments and cultural differences. The conversation moved slowly, filled with cautious questions and measured replies. Ajay held his teacup tightly, his fingers trembling slightly as he watched the two families interact.

Sana, though nervous, answered questions with a calm smile, masking the whirlwind within her. She wanted to make a good impression, to show them she could belong. But the weight of being judged silently began to press on her.

As the visit wore on, it became clear—this meeting was more than just tea and talk.

Finally, Ajay's father spoke. His deep, firm voice cut through the quiet. "Sana," he said, "you seem like a good girl, and your family is respectable. But I must speak honestly. You are a modern girl, full of dreams and ambitions for the outside world. I can see that in you."

Sana's heart skipped a beat.

"In our family, we value simplicity. We believe a daughter-in-law's primary duty is to care for the home. We would not allow her to work or pursue a career outside. I don't think you would be happy giving up your dreams for a life like that. And it would not be fair to expect it of you."

Sana's throat tightened. His words were not just a refusal—they were a rejection of her identity.

Ajay couldn't hold back anymore. "Papa, this isn't about traditions or roles. It's about love! Why can't you see that Sana and I can build a life together, even if it's different from what you imagined?"

His father shook his head. "Ajay, you're young and blinded by your feelings. Love alone doesn't sustain a marriage. It takes shared values, understanding, and alignment with family traditions. This match won't work. I won't allow it."

The silence that followed was heavier than before. Sana's parents rose quietly, their faces composed but disappointed.

Ajay walked them to the door, his heart breaking with every step. As they reached the entrance, Sana turned to him, her voice soft and trembling.

"Ajay, I truly hoped you would take a stand today. I needed you to speak for us, for me. But you didn't."

Her eyes shimmered with emotion; her pain evident but her tone gentle. "Your father is right in one way—I wouldn't be happy living a life that demands I give up who I am. And your family would never be happy with a daughter-in-law who doesn't fit their world. I don't want to be the cause of more conflict."

Her voice cracked slightly as she continued, "But what hurts the most is that you didn't fight for me. You let their silence speak louder than your love."

Ajay opened his mouth to speak, but no words came. He looked down, defeated.

Sana looked at him one last time, her heart aching. "Maybe this is where we let go. Sometimes, love isn't enough."

She turned and walked away slowly, her back straight, but each step felt heavier than the last. Inside, she was shattered. The pain of losing him, of not being chosen, cut deep. She had dreamed of a future with Ajay—a life full of love, laughter, and partnership. But now, that dream lay broken at her feet.

Back inside, Ajay's father stood resolute, unmoved. Ajay sat alone in the silence that followed, torn between love and loyalty, but fully aware of the price he had just paid.

That evening marked not just the end of a meeting, but the quiet collapse of a love story. Two hearts, full of dreams, collided with the reality of traditions too strong to bend.

And though Sana walked away in silence, her silence was louder than any words—echoing the pain of not being fought for, and the strength it takes to let go when love isn't returned with the same courage.

It was the end of their story, but the beginning of hers. She wasn't strong—not yet. The pain had consumed her. Her laughter faded, and her world lost its colour. She respected the elders' decision, but in her heart, she had wished for Ajay to rise for her, to choose her over the weight of customs. When he didn't, something inside her broke.

It would take time—maybe months, maybe years—for her to heal. For now, she carried only pain, and a love story that never found its ending.

"In his silence, I heard the loudest goodbye—a love left unspoken, echoing through the emptiness of my heart."

Chapter 7

The Goodbye That Broke Everything

Sana returned home completely shattered. Her family, deeply upset by the events, felt helpless watching her break into pieces. She walked straight into the bathroom, heart heavy and trembling, and stared at her reflection in the mirror. Her lips quivered as tears began to fall. "Why?" she whispered to herself. "Why did this happen to me? Why didn't he fight for our love? Why has God been so unfair to me?"

Her eyes searched for answers in the glass, but all she could see was a girl who gave her all and got silence in return.

For days, Sana locked herself in her room. She barely ate, barely slept. The vibrant girl who once lit up every room now sat quietly in the shadows.

She prayed with all her heart, hoping that things would eventually improve and that Ajay's parents would accept her with open arms. But despite her hopes, nothing seemed to change. Meanwhile, Ajay spoke to his mother in earnest, begging her to help convince his father. Yet, in his house, no one had the courage to go against his father's wishes.

Sana's family, heartbroken by her condition, decided to give her space to grieve. Her mother left plates of food at her door. Her father sat in the living room, sighing deeply every time he heard no movement from her side of the house.

Ajay, on the other hand, was no better. He was consumed with guilt and sorrow. He hadn't stopped thinking about her—her smile, her dreams, her courage. He hated himself for staying silent, for letting fear dictate his actions, for not standing up to his family when Sana needed him the most.

Sana was angry—not just at him, but at herself too. She kept questioning everything. *Why did he choose to love me if he knew his family would never accept me? Why did he dream with me if he didn't have the courage to protect those dreams? Did he ever truly love me?*

Two long weeks passed. Then, one night, Ajay finally gathered the courage to call her. His voice was shaky and low. "Sana... I'm so sorry, my love. I couldn't fight for us. I failed you." His voice broke, and she could hear his muffled sobs on the other end.

Sana closed her eyes as tears fell again. She still loved him, but love wasn't enough anymore. Taking a deep breath, she steadied herself. "Ajay, don't cry. Please. Your parents aren't wrong. Maybe they see something we don't. Maybe love isn't enough for a marriage. If our differences make us unhappy now, they'll only get worse later. We'll hurt each other more. What's the point?"

Her words cut deep—not just for Ajay, but for herself too. Yet she kept going.

"It's better we part ways now than live a life filled with pain and regret."

Ajay listened in silence, unable to argue. Her words made sense, but every syllable felt like a blade. Sana continued, voice shaking but firm. "Ajay... this is going to hurt. But we've got to let go. Crying and clinging to what could've been will only make it harder. Maybe this is God's way of protecting us from a bigger heartbreak. Let's move on. Let's try."

Ajay's breath hitched. "I know you're right," he whispered. "But it's tearing me apart, Sana. I don't know how to imagine my life without you."

There was silence. Heavy, suffocating silence. Each one waited for the other to take it back. To say, *Let's not give up.* But neither of them did.

Finally, Sana spoke again. Her voice was almost a whisper, yet steady, like someone who had cried enough and had no more tears left. "Ajay, no more talking. Please. Let's say goodbye now before we lose the strength to do it. I wish you all the happiness in the world. Goodbye, Ajay."

Ajay wanted to scream, to beg her to stay. But his guilt, his failure, and his silence held him back. "Goodbye, Sana," he said, barely audible.

The line went dead.

Sana sat by the window that night, tears streaming down her face, clutching her knees to her chest. Her heart ached, but she didn't allow herself to fall apart. Ajay's silence had answered all her questions. His love might have been real, but his fear was stronger.

Ajay stared at his phone, motionless. He had lost the one person who truly saw him. And the worst part was—he knew it was his fault.

That night, the pain of separation wrapped around them like a thick fog. It wasn't anger or hatred that broke them—it was silence, fear, and the weight of expectations.

Weeks turned into months. The ache in Sana's heart dulled, but it never truly disappeared. Her family stood by her, their support a silent shield around her. Still, the memories refused to fade—his voice, his smile, the dreams they painted together.

But Sana refused to break. She wouldn't let a man's silence define her worth. She didn't cry in front of anyone. She carried her heartbreak like a quiet strength.

Ajay, meanwhile, was a hollow version of himself. Every day, he replayed the moment he didn't speak up. The guilt clung to him, eating away at his spirit. He had always been the obedient son, the silent one. But in losing Sana, he realized how much that silence had cost him.

One cool evening, Sana sat on the balcony, staring at the full moon. The wind touched her skin gently, but her heart was restless. Her father walked up with a cup of her favorite coffee. "Sana," he said softly, "can we talk?"

She nodded and took the cup. He sat beside her, watching her carefully. "What have you decided, beta? It's been four months."

Sana looked down, her fingers wrapped around the warm mug. "I'm trying, Papa," she whispered. "But his memories... they follow me everywhere. I feel betrayed. He chose to love me. He made me dream. Then, when it mattered most, he said nothing. How do I forget that?"

Her father gently stroked her hair. "Beta, sometimes healing means stepping away from the things that hurt us. Why don't you go abroad? Your cousin, Mahi is in Sydney. You wanted to study child psychology. Maybe this is the sign to start again."

Sana hesitated. A part of her still hoped for a miracle. But another part knew that staying here meant staying stuck.

Tears filled her eyes, but she nodded slowly. "Maybe you're right, Papa. Maybe it's time to stop holding on."

That night, Sana made a decision. Leaving wouldn't erase the pain, but it might help her find herself again. And sometimes, loving someone meant letting them go—so they, too, could learn what they lost when they chose silence over love.

"When love feels like a lie, every unspoken word becomes the fuel for a new beginning."

Chapter 8

Where Dreams Begin Again

After two months, there was still no news from Ajay. He must be busy with his new job, Sana thought to herself. Before their separation, he had been selected by a well-known company—a moment that should have been celebrated together, but now felt like a distant memory.

Sana was preparing to leave for Sydney in ten days. The paperwork and formalities were nearly complete, and her bags were almost packed. A part of her longed to see Ajay one last time, to hold on to what little was left of their connection. But she stopped herself. Seeing him again would only make it harder to let go.

The day of her departure arrived. The airport was bustling, with trolleys rolling over tiled floors and announcements echoing in the air. Yet, Sana felt a strange stillness within her, as if her heart had paused in the middle of a sentence. Her mother's eyes were moist as she hugged her goodbye, but Sana smiled gently, not wanting to add more weight to the farewell.

As the plane ascended, she stared out the window, watching her world grow smaller and smaller. She couldn't help but wonder if she was leaving behind the last fragments of who she used to be.

After a long, exhausting flight, Sana finally landed in Sydney. The fatigue of the journey tugged at her body, but the sight of her cousin Mahi at the arrival gate brought a flicker of relief.

"Hi, Mahi! It's so nice to see you after so long," Sana said, her voice carrying a faint smile.

"It's been ages!" Mahi replied, embracing her tightly and taking the trolley. "You've lost weight. And your eyes... they look tired."

Sana just smiled, brushing it off. "Jet lag."

As they drove through the city, Sydney buzzed with life. The tall skyscrapers reached for the skies, the harbor sparkled under the sunlight, and the iconic Opera House stood as a testament to the city's charm. The sights should have thrilled her, but instead, Sana felt a bittersweet ache. It was a city of possibilities, a place where dreams could come alive—but hers had been shattered.

That night, as the city glowed with vibrant lights and the air buzzed with music, Sana stood by the window of her cousin's apartment. The liveliness of Sydney contrasted sharply with the heaviness in her heart. She once dreamed of a future with Ajay—a life filled with laughter, love, and togetherness. Now, those dreams were gone, and so was the lively, bubbly girl she used to be.

"Sana," Mahi said softly, walking in with two mugs of tea. "Aunty told me about Ajay and your relationship. I'm sorry."

Sana took the mug with a gentle nod.

"I know how hard it is to move on. It takes a lot of courage to start fresh like you have. I don't have the right to judge you or your love, but I feel like maybe you both gave up too soon."

Sana stayed silent, her chest tightening as the words sank in. Pretending to be strong wasn't always easy, and in that moment, she felt like the weight of it all might overwhelm her. She looked down at the tea in her hands, watching the steam swirl upward like a fading memory.

But deep down, she knew she couldn't allow herself to break again.

Sana enrolled in the University of Sydney's Master of Education (Child Psychology) program, hoping to turn her pain into purpose. The university's historic sandstone buildings stood tall, their arches and courtyards exuding a timeless elegance. Around her, the campus buzzed with life—students with big dreams and unrelenting determination filled every corner. The energy of the place was infectious, and for the first time in months, Sana felt the faint stirrings of excitement.

The next day marked her first day at the university. She stood before the mirror, pulling on a crisp white shirt and a pair of tailored denims. Her look was simple, yet classy—formal enough to feel confident, but relaxed enough to blend in. She applied a dash of kajal and let her hair fall loose over her shoulders. A quiet whisper escaped her lips, "Let's do this."

The crowd on campus was vibrant, filled with people from different walks of life, each carrying their own aspirations. As she walked through the halls, surrounded by the hum of conversations and the shuffle of hurried footsteps, Sana felt a tiny glimmer of hope. Maybe this was her chance for a fresh start.

Her eyes wandered to a couple sitting under a tree, laughing over coffee and notes. The sight tugged at her heart. For a moment, her mind drifted back to the garden bench where Ajay once sat beside her, sketching her name with a stick, on wet mud after the rains. She blinked away the memory, grounding herself in the present.

Her goal was clear now. She wanted to work with children, to help them navigate the complexities of their emotions and struggles. Perhaps, by guiding them, she could not only create a brighter future for them but also find a way to heal herself. The thought of making a difference in young lives gave her a sense of purpose that had been missing since her separation from Ajay.

In lectures, she sat with unwavering focus. She jotted down notes, asked questions, stayed back to clarify concepts. Her professors began to notice her sincerity. A classmate, Natalie, once remarked, "You've got such calm energy. You'll make a great child psychologist."

Sana smiled, genuinely this time. "That's the dream."

Sana poured herself into this new chapter, determined to make her pain count for something greater. She clung to the hope that by dedicating herself to her studies and her dream, she could distract her heart from the memories that still lingered like shadows.

Sydney, with its towering skyscrapers and sparkling harbor, stood as a city of endless possibilities. Yet, for Sana, it wasn't just about the city or the university—it was about finding herself again. And though the lively, chirpy girl she used to be still felt distant, she hoped that, in time, she could rebuild the pieces of her heart, one step at a time.

"Some goodbyes don't echo with words. They echo in the silence of two hearts still beating for each other, miles apart."

Chapter 9

A Heart That Never Moved On

Six months had passed, and life in Sydney had started to settle into a routine for Sana. She focused on her studies and assignments, diving deep into her coursework to keep herself occupied. Slowly, she began to feel more like herself again. She made a few friends at the university, and their company brought moments of laughter and lightness. Her cousin Mahi became her biggest support, always there to lift her spirits and encourage her to keep going.

But even with all the positive changes, there were days when Sana felt a hollow ache inside. Whenever she had a quiet moment, her thoughts drifted back to Ajay. Was he doing, okay? Did he get married? Was his job everything he hoped for? These questions swirled in her mind, unanswered but persistent.

There was no contact between them, yet Sana felt an invisible thread connecting their hearts. She knew Ajay well enough to sense that moving on wouldn't be easy for him either. The thought both comforted and saddened her, leaving her feeling incomplete, as if a piece of her life was missing.

Mahi tried her best to keep Sana engaged, taking her out to explore Sydney's vibrant streets or helping her with her studies. They shared late-night talks and heart-to-heart conversations, but even Mahi could see that a part of Sana still lived in the past.

Sana had changed. She wasn't the same bubbly, carefree girl she once was. She had learned to smile again, but there was a weight behind her eyes that never quite faded. Her dreams for the future were reshaping, yet the shadow of her lost love lingered, a quiet reminder of what could have been.

There were nights she'd lie awake, staring at the ceiling, wondering if she had made the right choice. Her heart knew the answer, but her mind still battled the memories. Healing wasn't linear—it came in waves. And every wave carried a bit of Ajay with it.

Sydney had given her a fresh start, a chance to rebuild her life. But even amidst the city's energy and her new friendships, Sana couldn't shake the feeling that something—or someone—was missing.

On the other side, Ajay had lost the spark that had just started to shine a year ago. His world was in pieces, and he couldn't imagine how life would ever feel normal again. As the only child of his parents, he didn't rebel or fight back. Instead, he withdrew into silence, burying himself in his new job.

He and Sana had once dreamed of a beautiful future together; weaving stories of what life would be like. But those dreams were now broken beyond repair.

"She must think I'm a coward for not fighting for us," Ajay thought helplessly as he stared out of the window, his chest heavy with regret.

Both of them were drowning in the pain of losing each other. Ajay's parents, oblivious to his heartache, insisted he get married. They searched for a simple girl from their community, convinced it was the right thing for him.

Ajay felt trapped. The walls of his home, once familiar, now felt like a prison. He wanted to run far away. "How can I love someone else? Sana is my one and only love. She'll always be. Marrying another girl would be unfair to her and to me. They can force me to marry, but they can't force me to love," he whispered to himself, his voice breaking with the weight of his pain.

It had been a year since they parted, yet not a single day went by without them missing each other. He knew Sana was in Sydney, pursuing her career, and the thought brought him a bittersweet sense of ease. It comforted him to believe she had moved on, even if his own heart remained tethered to her. The longing was relentless, but he convinced himself that silence was kinder than reopening wounds that could never fully heal.

Ajay had resisted the idea of marriage with every ounce of his being, but his mother's emotional pleas finally broke him. Defeated and torn, he found himself standing outside Sana's house, seeking solace. He spotted her mother sitting in the small garden, tending to her plants. She looked up, startled to see him after so long—a whole year had passed.

"Aunty," he greeted softly, his voice heavy with pain. She stood and hugged him tightly, her earlier anger melting away at the sight of his broken state.

"What's wrong, beta? You look completely shattered," she asked, her concern evident.

"Aunty, how is Sana?" he whispered before breaking into tears.

She sighed, understanding the depth of his sorrow. "Sana is in Sydney, pursuing her dreams. She's happy there, beta. Sometimes, life doesn't give us what we want. It's time for you to move on too."

Ajay shook his head, his guilt spilling out. "Aunty, I came to see you because I feel I'm betraying my love. My parents are forcing me to marry someone I don't know, someone I don't love. I can't do this. I can't do this to Sana... or to myself." His voice cracked, his emotions overwhelming him.

Sana's mother held his hand firmly, her eyes filled with sympathy. "Ajay, life doesn't always go the way we hope. Maybe God has a plan for you that you can't see right now. Trust that things will fall into place."

"I'm sorry, Aunty," he murmured, lowering his head. "I had no one else to turn to. No one understands this pain."

Her heart ached for him, but she stayed strong. "It's okay, beta. Just trust the path ahead. Do what you must, and give life a chance."

Ajay felt a sliver of relief, even amidst his turmoil. He bent down to touch her feet in gratitude before walking away, his steps heavy as he returned to face the storm waiting at home.

"Some love stories don't end with goodbye. They live on—in silence, in memories, and in hearts that never stop waiting."

Chapter 10

Stillness Between Heartbeats

Sana's mother gently told her that Ajay had come to meet her and shared the news of his marriage. For a moment, Sana sat still, absorbing the words. A strange wave of emotions surged through her—shock, pain, a quiet ache—but somewhere within, a bittersweet sense of relief settled.

She forced a faint smile. "I'm glad he moved on," she said softly. And for the first time in months, the crushing weight of guilt that had haunted her seemed to ease just a little. Maybe now, he would have someone beside him who could offer comfort, companionship... something Sana had once wished to give him.

Back in India, Ajay had done what was expected of him. Being the only child, he had responsibilities—obligations that weighed heavier than love. His parents had sacrificed so much for him; now it was his turn to repay. He married a simple Brahmin girl chosen by his parents, not out of love, but to fulfill his duty as a son.

They shared a home, but not a bond. Their marriage was courteous, cordial even, but it lacked the intimacy of true companionship. Conversations were brief, emotions guarded. They performed the roles of husband and wife more out of formality than feeling. The warmth Ajay once felt with Sana never found space in this new chapter of his life.

Within a year, they had a son—a beautiful baby boy who brought unexpected joy to Ajay's otherwise hollow world. He named him *Neil*. Everything Ajay had ever missed in his own childhood—freedom, laughter, gentle understanding—he tried to pour into Neil's life.

Even in a marriage built more on duty than desire, Ajay gave his all as a father. But at night, when silence wrapped around him, he often found his thoughts drifting back to Sana. She remained etched in a corner of his heart, untouched by time, loved in silence.

Eight years passed...

Sana had transformed into a woman of strength and grace. The chirpy, bubbly girl who once wore her heart on her sleeve had matured into someone composed, resilient, and deeply rooted in her purpose. She now worked at a reputed clinic as a child psychologist in Sydney, collaborating with a close friend. The dream of opening her own clinic didn't feel far-fetched anymore.

Her days were full—therapy sessions, paperwork, planning—but no matter how structured her life had become, her nights were still haunted by memories of Ajay. His silence, his smile, his promises... they lingered in corners of her mind that even time couldn't reach.

She rarely laughed the way she used to. The sparkle had dimmed, not out of sadness, but because she had outgrown that carefree world. She had learned how to survive, how to build, how to let go. But some love stories don't end. They just get quieter.

Her parents continued to pressurize her to settle down and return to India. They didn't understand why she refused every proposal, why she avoided the subject entirely. She'd say, "I'm not ready," but the truth was—her heart still belonged to someone she never truly stopped loving.

In the quiet hours after work, Sana often sat by her window with a cup of tea, staring out at the city lights. To the world, she looked fulfilled. But she knew the truth—there was a corner of her heart that still longed for closure, still held on to a thread of hope she never dared speak aloud.

Then came the call that changed everything.

It was her mother again, but this time, her voice trembled. "Sana... Ajay's wife... she's no more. A sudden accident. She died on the spot. The little boy... he's just eight."

Sana couldn't breathe. Her fingers went cold, and for a moment, the world went silent around her. She leaned against the wall, closing her eyes, trying to steady herself. "Oh God," she whispered. Her chest tightened—not just out of shock, but out of a sorrow that she hadn't expected would hit this deep.

She had never met Ajay's wife, never seen the child, but her heart broke for both of them. For the little boy who'd lost his mother, and for Ajay, who would now face grief all over again. Even after all these years, her care for him hadn't faded. It had simply lived quietly in her soul.

Restless and filled with worry, Sana made a decision she hadn't planned on making so soon—she booked a flight to India. "I just need to see him once," she told herself. "Just once, to know he's okay." She didn't know what would come of it, or what she would even say if she saw him. But the pull in her heart was stronger than any logic.

Though Ajay was never in love with her, her absence left a hollow space in his life. She had been his partner, his companion in routine, and the mother of his child. Their bond might not have been romantic, but it was real in its own quiet way. Her sudden departure shook the very structure of his world—one he had grown used to, even if it was never built on love.

Sana's parents were both surprised and overjoyed when she returned. But Sana's heart was miles away, still caught up in the ache of knowing what Ajay might be going through.

That night, as she sat on the balcony staring into the quiet sky, her mother joined her.

"Don't start this all over again, Sana," she said gently, though there was firmness in her voice. "You've worked so hard to move on. Don't walk back into something that only brought you pain."

Sana looked down, tears threatening to spill. "But Maa… he's lost his wife. He has a little boy. How can I sit here and do nothing?"

Her mother sighed. "Because sometimes doing nothing is the bravest thing to do. Sometimes, silence is kinder than stirring up old wounds. You're not the same girl anymore. And neither is he."

Sana nodded silently, but her heart refused to agree. She was still bound to him—not by promises or expectations, but by a kind of love that simply refused to fade.

The next morning, she woke up with a quiet resolve. Sana decided to open her clinic here itself. For some time, Ajay's thoughts took a backseat as she immersed herself in finding the perfect space, navigating paperwork, and designing every detail of the clinic with care. The process demanded all her energy—and for now, that was exactly what she needed.

Within a few months, her clinic was ready—a beautiful space filled with colors, books, soft lights, and laughter. Her work with children earned her praise and recognition.

Every now and then, she would catch herself lost in thought... wondering how Ajay was coping. Wondering if the boy—Neil—looked like his father. She hadn't reached out, hadn't seen him. But that unspoken connection still pulsed, quietly, deeply, eternally.

She tried to convince herself that everything happens for a reason. That maybe their story wasn't meant to be. That maybe this was destiny's plan all along.

But on some nights, when the world went still, her heart would whisper... *"What if there's still something left?"*

And in that stillness, between heartbeats, she could almost hear his name.

---

*"Some bonds live on in silence,
etched in absence."*

Chapter 11

Silent Threads

On the other hand, Ajay was navigating his own storm. The loss of his wife had left a void that no words could fill, but the weight of the tragedy was even heavier for Neil. At just eight years old, Neil had been inseparably close to his mother. Her presence was his world—her lullabies soothed his fears, her laughter lit up their home. Her sudden absence didn't just leave a silence—it left a darkness that consumed him.

Neil withdrew into a shell, his once-bright laughter replaced by stubborn silence. He spent hours sulking in corners, his eyes searching for something that was no longer there. His grief found release in tantrums—loud, unreasonable, and utterly heartbreaking. He lashed out not from anger but from pain, a pain no child should ever carry alone.

Ajay's family watched helplessly as Neil spiraled further into his sadness. Each passing day left them more anxious, more desperate for a way to bring him back from the shadows.

"It's been ten months now," Ajay's mother said one evening, her voice low with worry as she glanced at Neil, who was curled up in a corner, clutching his mother's old scarf. "He's still not settled. Please, Ajay, find a good child counselor. Someone who can help us understand him and care for him better."

Ajay's heart clenched at her words. The guilt of not being able to ease Neil's pain gnawed at him daily. He sighed heavily. "You're right, Maa. I'll look for someone who can help." His voice was thick with emotion. The weight of being both father and mother to Neil was crushing, and some days, it felt like he was failing at both.

In another part of the city, Sana had finally opened her own clinic. After years of hard work and perseverance, she had built a space where children could heal, where their inner worlds could be understood with compassion and care. As a child psychologist, her empathetic approach and deep understanding of emotional trauma earned her trust quickly. Parents praised her, children found comfort in her, and her career was steadily climbing.

But beneath that professional success lay a quiet storm. No matter how far she tried to run, thoughts of Ajay crept in like uninvited guests. She missed him—in the silence of her evenings, in the laughter of the children she helped, and in the unhealed corner of her heart that still whispered his name.

"This is destiny," she would tell herself every time memories threatened her composure. "It was written long before us. Fighting it is futile." But some wounds don't fade, no matter how many years pass.

Back in Ajay's world, things took a sharp turn one afternoon. It had been a particularly hectic week at work, and Ajay barely had time to process anything beyond deadlines. But then his phone buzzed, and he froze when he saw the caller ID—Neil's school.

"Mr. Ajay," the voice on the other end was tense, clipped. "Neil has hit another child in class. We need you to come to the school immediately."

Panic surged through him. He left the office without a word, heart thudding with worry. When he reached the school, he found Neil sitting in the principal's office, his eyes red and swollen, tears running down his cheeks. His tiny body trembled as he refused to meet his father's gaze.

The other child's parents were furious. "This is unacceptable! Our son is hurt! What kind of upbringing allows this behavior?" one of them snapped.

Ajay's face flushed with shame and helplessness. He knew Neil's actions were rooted in unspoken grief, but how could he make others see that? How could he explain that the little boy sitting in the corner wasn't violent—he was simply broken?

"I'm sorry," Ajay said, his voice soft but sincere. "We've been going through a difficult time. Neil lost his mother recently. He's struggling, and we're trying to help him the best we can."

Eventually, the matter was settled, but the incident left a scar deeper than Ajay expected. That night, he sat beside Neil as he slept, the child's arms wrapped tightly around a framed photograph of his mother. Tear stains marked his cheeks.

Ajay felt a pain so sharp it made him breathless. "He misses her so much," he thought, blinking away his own tears. "And I don't know how to help him."

The next morning, unable to focus at work, Ajay opened his laptop and began searching for therapists. He scrolled aimlessly until a familiar name stopped him cold.

Dr. Sana Verma.

One of the top-rated child psychologists in the area.

His fingers stayed over the keyboard for a while, but then he pulled back. He picked up his phone, scrolled through his contacts, and stopped. His throat felt dry, and his heart was full of mixed emotions. *What if she didn't want to see him? What if meeting him again brought back all the pain she had tried to forget?*

Then his eyes went to Neil—quiet, distant, not the same boy he once was. Something inside Ajay changed in that moment.

His breath caught in his throat. For a moment, the world tilted. He stared at the screen, unmoving, heart racing. *Is she back? Why didn't she call? Does she know about Neil... about what happened?*

He sat still, overcome by a whirlwind of emotions. Part of him longed to see her again, to speak to her, to maybe, just maybe, find closure. Another part of him recoiled—*was she married now? Did she have a family of her own?*

Questions crowded his mind, but one thing was clear—she might be the only one who could truly understand Neil.

Maybe this wasn't just a coincidence. Maybe life was giving them one more chance. Not for love or the past—but for Neil.

With a deep breath and nervous hands, Ajay finally tapped the screen and saved her clinic's address.

He would take Neil to see her.

No pressure, no expectations—just hope.

Some scars aren't visible, yet they shape every word, every tear, every silence.

Chapter 12

New Beginnings: A Reunion of Hearts

The next day, Ajay and Neil went to Sana's clinic. The reception area felt warm and inviting, painted in soothing green tones. Tiny pots of plants decorated the corners, and the walls were adorned with pictures of smiling children. A sense of calm and positivity filled the room, complemented by the soft hum of laughter from kids. In one corner, a small table held colorful toys, and a little boy was engrossed in piecing together a puzzle.

Neil walked over and quietly joined the boy. His small hands reached for a puzzle piece, but his heart carried a heavy weight. The absence of his mother had turned his world upside down, and though he didn't yet have the words to express it, the pain felt too immense for someone so young. He clutched the puzzle piece, his fingers trembling, and tried to distract himself with the toy. But no matter how much he tried, he couldn't escape the sorrow in his heart.

Ajay watched his son from the corner of his eye, feeling the ache in his own chest. Every time he looked at Neil, he was reminded of the boy's lost innocence, the joy stolen by grief. Ajay longed to take away the pain, to fix everything, but he had no answers—only questions.

Just as Ajay was lost in his thoughts, the receptionist's voice broke through the quiet.

"Neil Sharma?" she called gently.

Ajay's heart skipped a beat. He watched Neil slowly turn toward him, those quiet, questioning eyes reflecting a fear Ajay knew all too well. He could see the uncertainty in Neil's small frame. This moment marked a new chapter for them both, a step toward healing, but it was impossible to deny the weight of what it meant. Would Sana understand their pain? Would this visit open old wounds neither of them was ready to face?

Every step toward that door felt like walking through a fog of emotions, heavy with anticipation and dread. Ajay's mind raced, his heart pounding, unsure of what to expect when he finally crossed that threshold.

The door opened, and their eyes met. Time seemed to stop. Sana stood up from her seat, her white doctor's coat a perfect blend of professionalism and grace. The warmth in her smile was like a balm, familiar and comforting. But it was also a jolt, a sharp reminder of a past that was both cherished and painful. Ajay felt his breath catch in his throat. There she was, standing before him as beautiful and poised as he remembered, but so much had changed in the years between them.

For a moment, it felt like the years had disappeared—those long, aching years that had kept them apart. The memory of their love surged forward like a wave. The laughter, the shared dreams, the unspoken promises they had once made—everything came flooding back. Yet, as quickly as it arrived, it was gone. The reality of their separate lives, the years of silence, crashed down on them, pushing the emotions back into a quiet corner.

Ajay gave her a soft, hesitant smile, his voice thick with a mix of nervousness and familiarity. "Hi, Sana. How are you?"

Sana's heart skipped a beat. Her composure faltered just for a second. Memories of their time together rushed in—memories that she had tried so hard to suppress, afraid of what they might stir. But she steadied herself, grounding her emotions. This was no time for sentiment. She had a job to do.

"Hello, Ajay," she said gently, her voice steady and calm. "I'm fine. How about you?"

Ajay hesitated for a moment, before motioning to Neil. "Sana, this is my son, Neil."

Sana's gaze shifted to Neil, her heart aching at the sight of him. His small frame was hunched, his head lowered, his small hands gripping his father's fingers tightly. The silence between them spoke volumes—Neil's eyes avoided hers, a silent plea for comfort that he couldn't express.

Sana's heart broke. She knelt down to his level, her voice soft and motherly. "Hi, Neil," she said, her tone gentle, inviting. She held her arms open to him, but Neil flinched, not sure what to make of her kindness. She didn't push him. She understood that some wounds were too deep to be healed by a simple hug. Instead, she smiled and stood back up, offering them seats. She knew that this moment wasn't just about him being here to talk. It was about healing—and that couldn't happen all at once.

She turned her gaze back to Ajay, her eyes soft but filled with understanding. "I think I know why you're here," she said softly, her voice gentle but firm.

Ajay nodded; his voice heavy with emotion. Sana's voice softened, filled with empathy. "I'm so sorry to hear about the loss of your wife. My mother told me about the tragic accident and how everything got shattered, but I didn't have the courage to call or meet you."

Ajay sighed deeply; his chest heavy with a grief that had become a part of him. "It happened so suddenly. One moment she was there, and the next... everything fell apart. Neil's taken it the hardest. He's so quiet now, withdrawn. I get complaints from school, from home... he's struggling, Sana."

Sana's heart swelled with compassion as she looked at Neil. She could see the weight of his pain in the way he sat, his gaze distant, lost in his own world. His grief was a silent scream, one that he didn't have the words to express. Sana wanted to reach him, to pull him from that dark place, but she knew that it wasn't her place to rush him.

"Ajay," she said softly, her voice steady, "we'll help him. He's not alone in this. And neither are you."

As the words left her lips, Ajay felt something shift inside him—a tiny spark of hope. The darkness that had enveloped him for so long seemed to lift just a little. The warmth in Sana's voice, the understanding in her eyes, ignited something he hadn't allowed himself to feel in so long—hope for healing, for renewal.

But even as he held onto that hope, Ajay couldn't ignore the ache inside of him. Seeing Sana again, after all these years, stirred emotions he wasn't prepared for. Their past, the love they had once shared, surged to the surface, and for a brief moment, Ajay wondered if there was a possibility of finding their way back to one another.

But not now, not when Neil needed him. His son's pain was his priority. Yet, as they sat there, talking quietly, Ajay realized that maybe—just maybe—there was hope for them all.

"Some reunions are the start of new beginnings."

Chapter 13

Too Close, Yet Too Far

Ajay let out a sigh of relief, feeling lighter knowing Neil was in good hands. He trusted Sana completely—not just as a professional but as someone who would go the extra mile for Neil and, perhaps, for him too. There were so many unsaid emotions swirling in his heart. As he drove home that evening, a thought lingered. *Was she married? She didn't seem like it. But she's still the same Sana I knew back in college—kind, beautiful, and full of life.*

The next day, Ajay received a call from the clinic. The receptionist informed him that some documents needed his signature before Neil's treatment could officially begin. He saw this as an opportunity—a chance to meet Sana alone if she had a moment to spare. His heart raced as he wrapped up work quickly and headed straight to the clinic.

When he arrived, the clinic was unusually quiet. The receptionist handed him the forms and directed him to Sana's room. As Ajay stepped into the room, the faint scent of vanilla greeted him, instantly stirring a wave of memories. It was her signature fragrance—the one that had lingered in his mind for years. For a moment, he stood still, letting the familiar scent pull him back to a time when everything felt simpler, when she was his world.

It instantly took him back to the carefree days of their youth. *This smell still drives me crazy*, he thought, a small smile tugging at his lips.

But soon, reality struck him. This wasn't the college Sana he could casually joke with. The situation was different now—more delicate, more complicated. Sana looked up from her paperwork, her eyes lighting up when she saw him. "Ajay, come in. Let's get these formalities done," she said warmly, gesturing to the chair across from her desk.

Ajay sat down, trying to steady his thoughts. There was so much he wanted to ask, so much he needed to say, but for now, he focused on the papers in front of him. The answers to his questions could wait—at least for a little longer.

Finally, all the formalities were completed. Sana looked up; her tone professional yet considerate. "Ajay, the sessions will be every alternate day, lasting two hours each. It's important that someone from your family accompanies Neil for the sessions to make him feel supported," she explained. "The first session is scheduled for tomorrow at 5 PM sharp."

Ajay nodded, absorbing the instructions. "I'll make sure someone is with him," he replied, his voice calm but carrying the weight of his responsibility. "Thank you, Sana, for everything." Her reassuring smile in return felt like a quiet promise that they were on the right path.

Before opening the door to leave, Ajay hesitated. A part of him wanted to turn back and ask all the questions that had been weighing on his mind. Slowly, he turned and looked at Sana. Their eyes met, and for a moment, the room felt heavy with unspoken words.

"How are you, Sana?" he asked softly. "And where are you staying these days?"

Sana smiled gently, her voice calm but knowing. "You already know, Ajay. I'm still staying in the same place."

Before he could say anything more, a knock at the door interrupted them. A patient stood there, waiting, and the moment slipped away.

On the way back home, Ajay kept wondering what she meant by "same place." *Is she staying with her parents? Has she not married yet?* Now this created more confusion than before. He didn't know why it mattered so much, but it did.

The next day was Neil's first session. Sana began the treatment with a warm, reassuring smile, her voice gentle and inviting. She knelt beside him, pointing to the toys and puzzles in the cozy therapy room. "This is your space, Neil," she said softly. "You don't have to say anything if you're not ready. I'm here to help you, little by little." Neil glanced at her, hesitant but curious, his tiny fingers fidgeting with a puzzle piece.

After settling Neil, Sana turned to Ajay with a mix of professionalism and concern. "Ajay, let's go over some details about Neil's sessions," she said. They moved to her desk, where she explained the process, including regular appointments and ways to support Neil at home.

Ajay nodded, his voice carrying the weight of his responsibility as a father. "I'll do whatever it takes, Sana. He's my everything. Just let me know how I can help."

Sana reassured him with a kind smile as they completed the paperwork together, united by a shared goal to help Neil heal.

Sana watched Neil quietly from a corner as he played in the therapy room. He worked on a puzzle but held a soft toy tightly in his little hand, as if it was his shield against the world. Her heart ached for him, his silence speaking volumes. She jotted down her observations and gently introduced him to art therapy. Handing him paints and a pencil, she knelt down and said softly, "Draw anything you feel like, Neil. Anything that makes you happy." She stepped away to give him space, her eyes lingering on him for a moment before leaving the room.

When she returned, her breath caught. On the sheet of paper, Neil had drawn a small child playing with his mother in a park. The child looked happy, the colors bright and vivid. But Sana could feel the deep pain hidden behind the innocent strokes—the longing for a love he had lost too soon. She sat beside him for a moment, her heart heavy, knowing how much healing he needed.

That night, as Sana lay on her bed, sleep refused to come. Her mind swirled with emotions, tangled between her love for Ajay and her concern for Neil. *It's so hard to see him right in front of me and not touch him, not talk to him like before*, she thought, her chest tightening. Life had changed so much. She couldn't even ask Ajay the questions that haunted her—about his pain, his feelings, or what was left of their past.

He must have loved his wife deeply, she thought, *and the grief must still be fresh. Neil's struggles must weigh heavily on him, making him more serious and distant. But what about us? Is there even an 'us' anymore? Or am I just a memory that fits conveniently into his need for comfort?*

She shook her head gently, brushing away the thought. Maybe she was overthinking. Maybe he was just broken and needed healing–like Neil.

Tears pricked her eyes as she closed them, holding onto the faint hope that time would somehow bring answers— and maybe, just maybe, bring them closer again.

"Sometimes the heaviest things we carry are the words we never say."

Chapter 14

Silent Words, Heavy Hearts

Ajay couldn't control his thoughts anymore. The feelings swirling inside him were too strong to ignore. After much hesitation, he decided to call Sana. He needed to see her—not in a crowded place, but somewhere quiet. A space where it could just be the two of them.

Taking a deep breath, he dialed her number.

"Hi, Sana. If you don't mind, can we meet this evening?" he asked, his voice calm but lined with nervousness.

Sana was surprised by his directness. It had been a long time since he'd asked her something like this.

Although her heart wanted this, but her mother's words—and the years of separation and pain—created hesitation at first. She took a moment before answering, torn between caution and the feelings she thought she had buried.

But then, her heart won.

"Yes, Ajay. Where would you like to meet?" she replied, composed yet curious.

"Maybe we can go for a short drive and talk on the way? Is that okay with you?" he suggested, hope and hesitation blending in his words.

She smiled faintly, her heart already racing. "Yes, that's fine. Pick me up from my clinic at 8 p.m."

As the call ended, a familiar flutter stirred inside her—the same butterflies she had felt years ago when they first started meeting. But why now? Why in private? Her mind ran wild with possibilities, equal parts nervous and intrigued.

The day at the clinic dragged endlessly. Her thoughts kept drifting back to Ajay. By the time her shift ended, her heartbeat echoed louder than usual.

At exactly 8 p.m., Ajay pulled up outside the clinic. He stepped out, scanning the doorway.

When he saw Sana walk out, his breath caught. Her long, wavy hair framed her face gracefully, and her pastel kurta accentuated her quiet elegance. But it was her eyes—once filled with unending mischief—that now held a calm, thoughtful depth. She walked with a poised confidence, her smile soft but guarded. In that moment, he realized it wasn't just her beauty he had missed—it was the way she had once made everything feel alive.

"Shall we?" he asked, opening the car door.

"Yes," she said gently, stepping in.

As the car moved, silence settled between them. But it wasn't awkward—it was heavy with things unsaid. They both knew this wasn't just a casual drive. It was a moment long overdue.

"Thanks for meeting me, Sana," Ajay began. "I've been on a roller coaster lately. One thing after another. I met your mother before my marriage was fixed. She told me you were doing well in Sydney... chasing your dreams. And today, seeing you at your clinic—it made me happy. I know how much this meant to you."

He paused, then added softly, "Sana... what does your husband do? And the kids? I'd like to know about your life now."

Sana turned to look out the window, silent.

"Sana... I'm asking you. Is everything okay?"

Her voice was steady, though her eyes shimmered with something deeper. "Ajay, life doesn't stop for anyone. What we had... it was special. But I had to move on. There were proposals, yes. But I said no—not because of the past, but because I wasn't ready. I needed to build a life on my own terms. And I did."

Her words were calm, almost too composed, like she was protecting herself from her own truth.

Ajay's chest tightened. "Sana... I didn't know," he said, his voice low. She smiled sadly, eyes revealing years of pain she never voiced.

He pulled over to the side of the road and turned to face her. For a moment, words failed him.

Tears rolled down her cheeks, quiet and uncontrolled—tears she had held back for far too long.

"You were busy with your world, Ajay," she whispered. "I didn't want to interfere in your life. But my mom kept telling me about you. I thought... at least one of us is happy."

Ajay's jaw clenched. "How could you think I was happy?" he asked, a storm brewing in his voice. "My parents emotionally blackmailed me into marrying someone I didn't love. But once I did, I treated her with respect—because it wasn't her fault. I thought you had moved on, too. Your mom spoke so proudly of you, I believed you were happy."

He looked away, then back at her with raw honesty. "Sana... what have you done? You're beautiful, successful, still young. Why did you let your life go by like this? This hurts me deeply. I know I'm responsible for a part of it."

"Don't feel sorry for me, Ajay," she replied, her tone steady but sharp. "I'm not broken. I'm self-made. I earn more than most women my age. I've built a career, I've helped people, I've found purpose. I didn't lose myself—I found a stronger version. Marriage is not the only goal, Ajay. Look at yourself—you've lived your life ticking boxes others created for you. Have you ever truly lived for *you*?"

Her words pierced like arrows—truths wrapped in pain and pride.

Ajay sat quietly, taking it all in. The cheerful, easygoing girl he once knew was gone. In her place was a woman—layered, guarded, resilient.

After a pause, Sana spoke again. "I'm sorry if I sound harsh. But life has a way of changing us. It breaks you, teaches you, and turns you into someone you never imagined you'd be. I'm ready to help Neil, if he's open to it. But only as a professional. Nothing else."

Ajay looked at her—really looked. And beyond the words, he saw everything she hadn't said. The betrayal. The heartbreak. The strength. And a love buried too deep to reach now.

The drive back was quiet. When they reached her house, Sana's mother saw the car from the window but said nothing. She knew Sana would speak when she was ready.

Sana reached home and quietly rushed to her room. She knew she had been straight forward—maybe even harsh—with Ajay. But she also knew she was right. She *was* strong. She *was* a self-made woman who had rebuilt her life from the ground up.

And yet, deep inside, she also knew the truth she rarely allowed herself to face. It wasn't just her ambition or independence that kept her away from marriage or relationships—it was fear.

A fear of rejection. A fear of being abandoned by someone she dared to love again. She had lost trust in the very meaning of love. What once felt magical now felt risky. Unsafe.

Behind her composed strength was a heart still healing, still searching for something she wasn't sure existed anymore.

"Some people don't leave scars. They leave maps— showing us all the places we should never lose ourselves in again."

Chapter 15

The Night I Couldn't Pretend

The next eight months changed everything. Neil showed visible signs of improvement. Now nine years old, Neil was no longer the angry, withdrawn boy who refused to speak. Therapy was gradually transforming him. Slowly but surely, he began to share his feelings, to untangle the pain he had buried deep within after the sudden loss of his mother.

For the first time in years, Ajay felt the weight on his chest lighten. He watched his son laugh again, talk about school, and even get excited about silly things like cricket and comic books. He owed this miracle to Sana.

Ajay's parents, who had once looked at Sana with disapproval, now viewed her with quiet respect. One evening, his mother even whispered, "We were wrong about her. She would've been perfect for you." But they both knew it was too late. Ajay didn't respond, but that night, he sat for a long time on the balcony, staring into the dark sky.

A quiet ache lived inside him—a mixture of regret and longing. He wondered how life might have looked if he'd had the courage to choose differently years ago.

Amid this slow progress, something unspoken simmered between Ajay and Sana. They kept things professional, never crossing the line. But with every session, every exchange, the connection they once shared gently resurfaced. It was never loud—it came like a whisper, a shared glance, a lingering silence.

He missed the silly texts, the way she touched his arm when she laughed.

There were days he wanted to stop her as she walked out and just say it—"I'm sorry. I was weak. I should've fought harder." But every time he opened his mouth, silence won.

She wasn't his anymore. And maybe she never would be.

At home, Sana never mentioned Ajay beyond the context of Neil's progress. But her mother, always observant, could see right through her. "Still pretending it's all professional?" she asked once, raising an eyebrow.

Sana only smiled, too tired to explain how deeply she was torn inside.

In her quiet moments, when the world went still, Sana would lie awake and ask herself questions she had buried for years.

Why do I keep pretending I'm over him?

Why do I wear this mask of strength when I'm breaking inside?

Yes, she had been strong, bold, and self-made. But the truth she never admitted—not even to herself—was that the reason she never opened up to love again was fear. Fear of rejection. Fear of being left out once more. She had lost faith in love the day Ajay didn't choose her. No matter how hard she tried to rationalize it, it still hurt.

She had never been afraid of being alone. She had always been afraid of being someone's second choice.

Love, she had learned, doesn't always arrive wrapped in perfect timing. Sometimes, it shows up when hearts are too bruised to receive it.

And still, hers kept choosing him in quiet, aching ways.

As Neil's therapy sessions reduced to just twice a month, the distance between her and Ajay felt harder to maintain. Each time they met, her composure cracked a little more. Her heart still recognized him as the one she had once dreamed of forever with—and it refused to forget.

On Christmas Eve, she tried to distract herself by attending a party with some old friends. But as the night wore on and the drinks took effect, the emptiness crept back in. Unable to resist, she called Ajay.

"Hello?" Ajay's voice came through, warm and alert despite the hour. "Sana? Are you okay? It's 1 a.m. You sound drunk. Where are you? Do you need me to come pick you up?"

His concern cracked something inside her. She had tried for so long to seem okay, to move on, but the walls she'd built were paper-thin now.

"Ajay," she whispered, her voice trembling, "why do you always sound like you care?"

She paused; breath unsteady. "You make it so hard for me to pretend. To act like I don't feel anything."

There was silence.

"I've tried, Ajay. I really tried to forget what we had, to bury everything... but tonight, I just can't. I thought I could live without you. I thought I was strong enough. But I was lying. To everyone. To myself."

A faint laugh escaped her lips, but it was bitter, sad.

"I still love you, Ajay," she said softly. "I never stopped. Every time I see you, every time I hear your voice, it's like my heart forgets all the reasons I tried to stay away."

She didn't wait for his response. Her truth had slipped out, and that was enough. She ended the call and curled up in bed, tears soaking the pillow.

The next morning, her head pounded with a dull ache. The events of the previous night replayed like a broken film reel.

What did I do? Did I really say that?

She sat up in panic, breath short. There was no hiding now. No undoing what had been said.

After a long moment of pacing and regret, she picked up her phone and dialed.

"Ajay? Good morning," she began, her voice unsure. "I'm... I'm really sorry for last night. I shouldn't have called you like that."

There was a pause before Ajay's voice came through, surprisingly calm.

"Good morning, Sana. How are you feeling now?" he asked gently. "You were quite drunk," he added with a small chuckle. "But honestly... I'm glad you called. It reminded me that behind the composed Sana is still the same girl who once loved me deeply."

Her heart skipped a beat.

She swallowed hard. "Can we meet for lunch today?"

"I have a meeting now, but I'll text you the place and time," he replied.

As she ended the call, Sana stood by her window, looking out at the city soaked in Christmas spirit. The truth was out. Her heart had spoken. There was no taking it back now.

And maybe, just maybe, that was okay.

---

*"When love spills after silence, it's never a mistake—
it's a truth set free."*

Chapter 16

The Silence That Said It All

Sana's phone buzzed, and her heart skipped a beat when she saw Ajay's text:

"I want to take you to a special place for lunch. Be ready by 12 noon. I'll pick you up near your clinic."

Butterflies fluttered in her stomach as she read his message. She took a deep breath, trying to steady her emotions. Her mind raced with thoughts, torn between her feelings and her sense of boundaries. A part of her longed to run to him, to hold him close and whisper, *"I need you, Ajay. Life feels impossible without you."* But another part of her held back, reminding her of his responsibilities as a father and the complexities of his life.

She stared at her reflection in the mirror, wondering if her eyes still carried that same innocence he once fell for—or if time had carved too many cracks.

"Don't expect anything," she whispered to herself. "Just go, listen, and leave with dignity."

By 12 sharp, she was at the clinic, waiting. Ajay was already there, leaning casually against his car, his presence commanding attention.

She paused as her eyes found him—tall, confident, and composed in a way that made the world around him blur. In that moment, a wave of memories washed over her. It felt like yesterday when she had first met him at the college fest—a quiet, introverted boy with a deep love for coding and a world hidden behind his calm eyes. He was the kind who preferred staying behind the scenes, spending hours lost in lines of code rather than in conversation.

But today, the boy she once knew had transformed into a self-made man. Ajay was now working at a leading multinational tech firm, heading major projects, and known for his sharp intellect and innovative thinking. He had turned his passion into purpose and built a name for himself in the world of technology.

Yet despite all his success, it wasn't the job titles or polished charm that pulled her in. It was the way he still looked at her—like time hadn't changed a thing. Like he still remembered everything.

From the boy who lived a modest life in a small house and embraced simplicity, was now someone who lived in quiet luxury—without letting it define him. A sleek black car, an elegant sense of style, and the kind of presence that turned heads without trying—his growth was admirable, but what struck Sana most was that the core of him still felt the same.

He wore a black shirt that hugged his broad shoulders perfectly and black trousers that gave him an effortlessly refined look. His neatly combed hair and confident stance exuded a quiet charm.

When his eyes met Sana's, he paused, taken aback for a moment. She looked radiant in a crisp white shirt tucked into well-fitted denim, a look that was simple yet breathtaking. Her hair, still curled from the previous night's party, was tied back in a high ponytail, framing her glowing face. Her cheeks carried a soft, natural blush, and the subtle vanilla scent of her perfume lingered in the air as she approached, every step graceful and composed.

He wanted to say something—anything—but the lump in his throat betrayed him. He had rehearsed this moment, but none of his words felt enough now.

As Sana slid into the passenger seat, Ajay's carefully composed thoughts unraveled. He had planned to speak, but her beauty left him at a loss for words.

"Hi, Ajay. Thanks for meeting me on such short notice," she said softly, her voice as gentle as her presence.

Ajay exhaled, grounding himself in the moment. "You're welcome, Sana," he replied with a warm smile. As he looked at her, he saw not just beauty but a quiet strength in the way she carried herself.

"Where are we going, Ajay? You said it's a special place," Sana asked, curiosity and a hint of nervousness in her voice.

Ajay glanced at her with a soft smile. "Just relax, Sana. Enjoy the beauty around us. It will take some time, but I promise, it'll be worth it."

She let out a small sigh. "Can we talk on the way? I feel embarrassed about how I behaved last night."

Ajay's expression turned gentle. "Sana, it's okay. When we bury our emotions for too long, they find a way out. But I am worried about you. Are you really happy? You left India, chose to be alone... don't you feel lonely?"

His words touched something deep inside her. She kept looking out the window, avoiding his gaze.

"Lonely?" she repeated in her mind. "There are nights when silence feels louder than the world outside."

Ajay continued, his voice almost a whisper. "I know, Sana. You still have feelings for me. Your words from last night are still in my heart."

Sana clenched her hands, forcing a smile. She didn't want to ruin the moment. This time with him felt precious, and she knew the truth—no matter how much she loved him, life had already made its choices.

She felt exposed, vulnerable—almost foolish. What if Ajay took last night's confession as a sign of weakness? That scar of rejection he had left behind still lived in her soul, quietly reshaping the woman she had become. The Sana he once knew—the cheerful, open-hearted girl—had long been replaced by someone guarded, someone who had built her strength out of pain.

Forgiveness came easily to her for most people. But Ajay... he was the quiet ache she had learned to live with. Not out of bitterness, but because some endings leave questions that time alone can't answer.

She turned slightly toward him, her voice quiet but steady. "Ajay... I need to tell you something I've never said out loud."

He glanced at her, attentive and silent.

"I became strong because of you," she said, her gaze fixed on the road ahead. "Not just because of your presence, but because of your absence too. Because of that silence you left me in... it hurt, Ajay. It changed me."

Ajay remained still, his hands tightening slightly on the steering wheel.

"I'm not saying this to blame you," she continued softly, "but because that pain shaped me. It made me build walls, find my footing again... but a part of me—" she paused, struggling to hold back the emotion, "—a part of me still remembers how I once looked at you like you were my whole world."

Her voice dropped, almost a whisper now.

"And now, sitting beside you again after all these years... I hate that I still feel that same pull. You're still my weakness, Ajay. And that scares me more than anything."

He didn't speak, but something in the air shifted—thicker now, heavier with the weight of everything left unsaid for too long.

"The heart breaks in silence, yet finds the strength to love again."

Chapter 17

Between the Pages of Our Love

Soft melodies played in the background, stirring something deep within Sana's heart. Each note seemed to echo the quiet ache she'd buried over the years—love, loss, and longing wrapped in a symphony of memories she'd tried so hard to forget. She closed her eyes for a second, letting the music wash over her like a familiar, bittersweet friend. The road stretched endlessly ahead, mirroring the journey of her own life—long, uncertain, and filled with twists that had shaped her into someone she no longer fully recognized.

After an hour and a half, the car finally slowed. As Ajay parked, Sana stepped out and gasped softly. "Wow... this place is incredible," she whispered, her voice carrying both awe and vulnerability. "I've never been here before."

It was unlike any place she had ever seen—peaceful, untouched by the noise of the world. A breathtaking lakeside restaurant, nestled between towering trees and blooming flowers. A stone path wound through the lush greenery, leading to an open dining area where wooden tables sat beneath twinkling fairy lights. The air was filled with the sweet scent of fresh earth and jasmine, while the soft sound of water rippling in the lake played in harmony with the gentle hum of romantic music.

A wooden deck stretched over the shimmering lake, offering the perfect view of the golden reflections dancing on the water. Ducks glided lazily, unaware of the passage of time, while a cool breeze wrapped around Sana, carrying whispers of memories she had fought so hard to silence.

She ran her fingers through her loose curls, inhaling deeply. For the first time in years, she felt something stir inside her—a warmth she had forgotten, a reminder of the girl she once was before life had hardened her into who she was now. Yet, despite the surge of emotions, she stood tall, composed—strong, self-sufficient. She had learned to survive heartbreak, to rise above her past, and to build a life from the shattered pieces of herself. But that part of her—the woman who once allowed herself to dream of a future with Ajay—still lingered, buried beneath the surface.

Ajay was her weakness. As they stood there, Sana fought the overwhelming desire to surrender to the moment. She wanted to forget the pain, the years of distance, and just live in the warmth of what they once had—the passion, the laughter, the carefree love. She wanted to feel as she did eight years ago, when their world was full of fun, romance, and dreams. But the reality of her life now—the responsibilities, the pain, the years of heartbreak—kept her tethered to a past that was too heavy to shed.

Ajay had already reserved a table in the quietest corner, away from prying eyes. He pulled out a chair for her, his gaze soft but searching. She smiled—a small, hesitant smile that didn't quite reach her eyes.

As she settled into the seat, Ajay leaned forward, his voice gentle yet firm. "Sana, let's talk before we order lunch."

Her heart clenched. She had spent years building walls around herself, convincing the world—and herself—that she had moved on. But sitting across from him, in this tranquil, almost dreamlike place, those walls felt as fragile as paper.

She took a deep breath, gathering the courage to speak the words that had been buried for so long. "Ajay, this isn't easy, but I'll still try." She looked down, her fingers tracing the rim of her water glass. "When we parted ways years ago, I was completely shattered. I lost my trust in love, in relationships. A part of me was angry with you... because you never fought for us. And another part of me wanted to step away so you could move on. But in doing that, I lost myself. I forgot who I was, what my heart truly wanted."

Her voice wavered, but she didn't stop. The pain had lived inside her for so long, making her stronger, yet leaving a hollowness she couldn't fill. "I kept myself busy—studies, work, success—but no matter what I did, something inside me always felt empty. I had a small hope, a foolish hope, until the day you got married. And when that hope broke, I broke too."

She looked away, trying to hold back the tears threatening to spill. "I'm happy you moved on, Ajay. I really am. And I tried too. But I could never let anyone else come close to me. I just couldn't. Because no matter how much I fought it, I have only ever loved you."

Ajay's breath hitched, his fingers tightening around the edge of the table. He wanted to say something, to reach for her hand, to tell her what was in his heart—but before he could, she continued.

"But things are different now. We can't go back. We have responsibilities. You have Neil, and I have my work. What we feel... it's just a dream, a fantasy. And we both know dreams don't last forever."

Her voice cracked slightly at the end, but she quickly straightened, forcing a small, painful smile. "So let's just enjoy this lunch, Ajay. Let's pretend, just for today, that nothing has changed."

She looked at him, searching his face for a reaction, but he remained silent, his eyes dark with emotions he couldn't express. In that heavy silence, they both knew—the past was gone, but the love between them still lingered, unspoken and unresolved.

After a delicious lunch and delightful desserts, they strolled through the garden by the lake. The garden was serene, quiet, with soft lights casting gentle glows over blooming flowers. The sound of water splashing against rocks and the rustling of leaves in the breeze created an atmosphere that was both peaceful and charged with emotion. Each step seemed to bring them closer, yet the space between them still felt impossible to bridge.

Ajay broke the silence. "Sana, I'm so sorry for all the loss we've faced. I know I can't bring back the past, but I still hope for a better future. I still love you—I've told you many times, and I'm not lying. Can we try to stay close, even if it's just as good friends? We're both lonely, and maybe we can share our joys and sorrows together."

Sana stopped walking, her eyes filled with both pain and strength. "Ajay, please understand," she whispered, her voice trembling slightly, "love and friendship are two very different things."

Her words, gentle yet firm, carried the weight of years of heartbreak and hard-won independence. Though the love between them still burned, Sana knew that protecting her heart meant drawing a clear line. The garden around them bore witness to their quiet sorrow, and the bittersweet hope of finding peace, even in the face of what they once had.

"At least, stay in my life—not just as Neil's therapist, but as my best friend," Ajay said, his eyes filling with unshed tears, his hands folded in a quiet, pleading gesture. Sana smiled softly, her fingers brushing against his. "Okay, Ajay, let's give it a try," she said gently.

As they made their way back to the car, they spoke of the time spent apart—some good moments, but also some painful ones. They shared their memories, and with each word, the weight in their hearts lightened, replaced by a quiet warmth. The road ahead no longer seemed as daunting. The heaviness of their past still lingered, but for the first time in a long while, they both believed that together, they could find a way to move forward.

The peaceful drive home felt like a new beginning; their hearts filled with a spark of hope they had long thought lost.

"Even in heartache, there's a whisper of hope, a new beginning waiting to unfold."

Chapter 18

The Echo Between Doubts and Desires

A year passed. Neil was now 10 years old. He had grown into a mature and sincere child. Over time, he slowly changed—his grades improved, and he became calmer, more balanced. He was a sincere boy who had learned that life was full of ups and downs. He still missed his mother every single day, but now, he had made peace with her absence. He believed she was in a better place, watching over him.

Neil had sharp eyes, just like Ajay's. He was fiercely protective of his father—maybe because life had been tough on him from such a young age. Sana could see this. She knew he wouldn't easily accept anyone taking a place in his father's life.

Meanwhile, Ajay and Sana found their way back to each other. They talked more, met often—lunches that turned into long dinners, movies that ended with hand-in-hand walks in the park. They visited their favorite restaurants, laughed over old memories, and lost track of time in deep conversations. Love was once again knocking on their hearts. The loneliness they had carried for so long now pulled them closer. They longed for each other, craved the warmth they once shared.

Sana's heart ached with memories. *I miss the way his hands felt on me, the way his lips tasted when he kissed me. Will I ever feel that again?* A sharp pain spread through her chest. The past was beautiful, but the wound of separation still bled deep inside her.

Lost in thought, tears slipped down her cheeks. A sudden knock on the door jolted her back to reality.

"Sana?" Her mother's voice broke her trance. She quickly wiped her face. "Come in, Maa."

Her mother stepped in, her sharp gaze scanning Sana's face. "I've been calling you for five minutes. What's wrong?"

Sana forced a small smile. "Just lost in some memories."

Her mother sighed and sat beside her. "Sana, I need to talk to you." Her tone was serious. "It's about Ajay. I hope you know what you're doing. He has a lot of responsibilities, and I don't want you to get hurt. Don't make a fool of yourself by investing in this relationship. If you break this time, it will be hard to get back on track." She paused, her voice turning colder. "You're playing with fire. Do you remember how his father spoke to you? They don't deserve a girl like you. And how do you know Ajay isn't just passing time for Neil's sake?"

Her words struck deep, forcing Sana to face the doubts she had been pushing away.

"How can someone love twice? I mean, he must have done all this with his wife, and now that she is no more, he's either passing time or returning to his old love. Where is the seriousness in a relationship? Sana sat on the balcony, staring at the sky. Her gut whispered warnings her heart didn't want to hear.

They still loved each other—that unspoken connection, the fire between them, hadn't faded. It didn't need words to be understood; it was there, lingering in every glance, every touch, every moment they shared.

Sana sat in silence, her mother's words echoing in her mind long after she had left.Doubt crept into her heart, but so did something stronger—her love for Ajay. She knew what they shared wasn't just a passing moment. It was real, deep, and impossible to ignore.

The next day at work felt ordinary. Neil's therapy sessions had reduced, and now he only visited the clinic once a month for a routine checkup. Ajay was also away for some official work, leaving Sana with time to think—about him, about them.

She missed him—his presence, the way he made her feel safe. But her mother's warning still echoed in her mind, making her hesitate. Was she making a mistake?

To distract herself, she focused on work. Next week, she had to attend an International Conference in Goa, a prestigious event where only the top 20 doctors in India were invited. It was an honor, but something felt off.

Lately, her efficiency had dropped. She had always been organized, sharp, and focused, but ever since Ajay came back into her life, she found herself distracted. He consumed her thoughts, making it hard to concentrate. Was he a beautiful distraction or a roadblock to her goals?

Deep down, her gut knew—she was falling for him. One part of her wanted to surrender completely, to let love wrap around her like it once did. But another part, bruised by the past, warned her: this could leave you in pieces again. Yet, despite it all, her first feeling won the battle.

She sighed deeply, shutting her laptop. The conference would be her escape. Or so she hoped.

Still, she couldn't deny the excitement. "Goa without Ajay will be boring," she thought, smiling to herself.

She texted him about the trip, sharing the details. Hours passed with no response. *Maybe he's busy*, she murmured, pushing the thought away.

As she was heading home, her phone rang. It was Ajay.

"You're going to Goa?" His voice was sharp, laced with something deeper.

"Yes," she answered, a little surprised by his tone.

"Which hotel? When are you leaving? Flight details?" He fired off questions one after the other, making her blink.

"Ajay, why so many questions?" she asked, half amused, half curious.

"Just tell me," He insisted.

Sana sighed and emailed him all the details. Only then did he seem to relax.

She smiled, shaking her head. This wasn't just curiosity. It was care, protectiveness—possessiveness. And deep down, she liked it.

Sana was excited about the Goa trip. She had always loved the place—it had a calming, almost therapeutic effect on her. The sound of waves, the salty breeze, the endless stretch of sand—it felt like an escape from reality.

But this time, something felt different. Without Ajay, it wouldn't be the same. A soft smile played on her lips as the thought crossed her mind.

She whispered to herself, "If his presence disturbs me, I need to gather the courage to walk away. But if his absence breaks me, I must fight for us."

"Goa is beautiful, but without him... it might just feel empty."

---

*"Love's return isn't easy—
it asks the soul to risk again."*

Chapter 19

Entangled in Desire

The following week, Sana arrived in Goa for a two-day international conference. The day was packed with back-to-back sessions, filled with panel discussions, keynote speeches, and networking. By the time it ended, exhaustion weighed heavily on her shoulders. Her heels pinched her feet, and even the strongest coffee had lost its effect hours ago.

She headed straight to her room—a stunning, sea-facing retreat tucked away in a quieter corner of the resort. As she stepped inside, the soft sound of waves crashing against the shore welcomed her, the salty breeze wafting in through the balcony doors. The subtle hum of the sea created a calm she hadn't felt in days. Despite her fatigue, the view was utterly mesmerizing.

The salty breeze of Goa wrapped around Sana as she stepped onto the balcony. The rhythmic crashing of waves filled the night air. Beach shacks sparkled in the distance, their lanterns swaying gently. Somewhere nearby, a guitarist strummed a soulful tune, blending with laughter, clinking glasses, and the scent of grilled seafood. The sea stretched endlessly, wild and free—just like her heart, just like her yearning.

Though she tried to focus on the presentation she had to present at the conference next day, her thoughts kept circling back to Ajay. His voice, his eyes, the way he touched her like she was the only woman in the world. He had a way of reaching the softest, most hidden parts of her, even without trying.

She sighed, hugging her arms around herself. "Uff, he's impossible to forget." A tired smile tugged at her lips, even as her heart ached with the heaviness of missing him.

Just then, a knock on the door made her jump. Frowning, she checked the time—it was past ten. Who could it be at this hour?

She opened the door—and froze.

Ajay.

He stood there, slightly damp from the humid air, shirt unbuttoned at the collar, the top few buttons open to reveal just a hint of his chest. His eyes were dark, unreadable, intense—burning with everything he hadn't said.

Her breath caught in her throat. "You... what are you doing here?" she whispered, her pulse hammering against her ribs.

"I couldn't stay away," he said, voice rough, low. "You left without saying a word. I had to see you."

Before she could respond, he stepped inside and shut the door behind him. The soft click echoed in the room, louder than it should have.

"You shouldn't be here," she murmured, even as her eyes betrayed her resolve.

Ajay's gaze pinned her to the spot. "Then stop me. Say it, and I'll walk away."

But she didn't. She couldn't.

His lips found hers in a kiss that was fierce and aching—like a dam breaking after holding back too much for too long. It wasn't just desire; it was everything they had buried, everything they had never said aloud. She gasped softly, her breath catching as he pulled her into him, lifting her with ease, pressing her back against the cool wall as the heat between them surged.

Her fingers tangled in his hair, desperate to hold on, as though afraid the moment might vanish. His mouth trailed down the curve of her jaw to the delicate skin of her neck, each kiss a spark, each breath against her skin like fire licking at her senses.

"I've missed you," he whispered, his voice trembled with emotion. "Every damn second."

"You drive me mad," she breathed against his ear.

"Then let me lose my mind with you."

They stumbled toward the bed, lips never parting. Their bodies tangled in desperate need, fueled by longing and frustration, by love and loss. Clothes fell to the floor like forgotten burdens. His hands roamed over her with reverence and urgency, as though trying to relearn the feel of her. She arched against him, her nails digging into his back, her soft sighs and moans mixing with the sound of the waves crashing outside.

He kissed every inch of her like he was drinking her in, memorizing her all over again. "You're in my veins, Sana," he murmured, voice thick. "I don't know how to breathe without you."

That night, nothing else mattered—no doubts, no fears, no rules. Just them.

The waves crashed outside, wild and relentless. Inside, their passion matched its fury—unapologetic and raw. They explored each other with renewed hunger, as though time apart had only deepened the craving. Every touch, every kiss, screamed of longing, pain, and love that had refused to die. Their bodies moved in rhythm, their hearts syncing with every breath, every whisper.

Goa didn't just bring them together. It set them ablaze.

Hours later, the room glowed in soft orange light as dawn approached. The curtains fluttered gently in the early breeze. The scent of saltwater, sea air, and him still clung to her skin.Sana stirred, her muscles sore in the most delicious way. Her skin still hummed from his touch. She smiled, feeling Ajay's arm wrapped protectively around her waist. His breath was steady against the curve of her neck, his presence anchoring her like nothing else ever had. For the first time in a long while, she felt complete. Not torn, not confused—just held.

She glanced at the time—conference round two started in an hour.

As she carefully began to shift, Ajay grumbled in protest, tightening his grip around her. "Where do you think you're going?" he mumbled, his voice thick with sleep and laced with possessiveness.

"I have to present today," she whispered, brushing her fingers gently through his hair.

"Cancel it," he murmured, eyes still shut.

Sana laughed softly. "I can't. It's kind of important."

He finally opened one eye, giving her a lazy grin. "Then at least kiss me like you mean it before you go."

She leaned in, their lips meeting in a slow, lingering kiss that promised more. So much more. A kiss that said *this isn't over. This can't be over.*

As she moved around the room, gathering her clothes, brushing her hair, slipping into her conference outfit, Ajay lay on the bed, watching her. His eyes didn't waver. It was like he was trying to capture every moment, etch it deep inside him so he wouldn't forget.

Something had shifted between them last night—not just physically, but soul-deep. The distance, the hurt, the misunderstandings—none of it mattered in that room, in that night. They had let go, surrendered to something bigger than their doubts.

And neither of them wanted to pretend otherwise anymore.

"Some love stories may fade, but they stay with us forever."

Chapter 20

A Love That Felt Like Home

As the sun dipped into the horizon, painting the sky in hues of orange and pink, Sana rushed to her hotel room. She had a flight to catch tonight, and there was barely any time to talk to Ajay.

"I hope he knows we have to leave," she murmured to herself.

But the moment she reached the reception, she froze.

Ajay was already there, standing with their luggage.

A sigh of relief escaped her lips. "Oh, thank God! You knew we had to catch a flight."

Ajay smirked, his eyes twinkling with mischief. "We're not going home, dear."

Sana blinked in confusion. "What? Why?"

He stepped closer, lowering his voice. "Because I'm extending this trip. We're staying in Goa for two more days, and I have a surprise planned for you. So, call home and inform them. No more questions."

Excitement bubbled in Sana's chest. She loved surprises. And Ajay? He loved spoiling her, making her smile, and making up for all the time they had lost.

They left the hotel and drove along a scenic coastal road, the salty breeze playing with her hair. The road twisted and turned, revealing glimpses of the sea, dancing under the golden twilight. Soon, they arrived at a luxurious beachside resort, nestled between swaying palm trees and the endless ocean.

Sana's breath hitched. It wasn't just a resort—it was magical. Each cottage stood right on the shore, private and secluded, with wooden decks leading straight to the soft, golden sand. The sound of waves crashing was the only music around, and the air smelled of fresh flowers and sea salt.

She turned to Ajay, eyes wide with shock. "Ajay, what is all this? Why are you doing so much?"

He pulled her closer, his fingers tucking a strand of hair behind her ear. "Because I want you to be happy. Because you deserve this. Now stop asking questions and just enjoy the moment."

Her heart swelled with love. This wasn't just a vacation. It was Ajay's way of telling her how much she meant to him—without saying a word.

As they stepped into their private sea-facing cottage, Sana's eyes widened in awe. The room was elegantly decorated with soft, sheer curtains swaying in the ocean breeze. A large glass door opened onto a wooden deck with an infinity pool, merging seamlessly with the vast Arabian Sea ahead. The golden glow of lanterns cast a romantic warmth over the space, and the faint scent of jasmine and sandalwood filled the air.

Sana turned to Ajay, still overwhelmed. "This is unbelievable."

Ajay chuckled, wrapping his arms around her from behind. "It's just the beginning, love."

The first evening was pure magic. They walked hand in hand along the moonlit beach, letting the cool water kiss their feet. The night sky was sprinkled with stars, and Ajay suddenly stopped, pulling her close.

"Close your eyes," he whispered.

Sana hesitated but obeyed.

A moment later, she felt something cold against her skin. A delicate anklet.

Her eyes flew open, and she gasped. "Ajay..." "I saw it and thought of you," he said softly. "Something to remind you of this night, always."

Her heart melted. It was these little things—his thoughtfulness, his love—that made her fall for him all over again.

The next morning, Ajay woke Sana up with a kiss on her forehead. "Rise and shine, sleepyhead. We have a long day ahead."

After a lazy breakfast on their oceanfront balcony, he revealed the first surprise—water sports!

Sana squealed with excitement as they went parasailing, soaring over the crystal-clear waters, hand in hand, hearts racing together. They jet-skied, screaming and laughing like carefree lovers. Ajay made sure she felt safe, protected, and adored.

By the afternoon, they were back at the resort, lounging in their private pool. The sun painted their skin in a golden glow, and Ajay couldn't take his eyes off her.

"You look beautiful," he murmured, trailing his fingers down her arm.

Sana shivered, feeling the electric pull between them. She leaned in, brushing her lips against his—soft at first, then deeper, more intense. The world faded, leaving only them, lost in the moment, lost in each other.

As the sun melted into the horizon, splashing the sky with shades of gold, crimson, and indigo, a gentle breeze carried the salty scent of the ocean, wrapping the evening in a dreamy embrace. Ajay and Sana made their way to a cozy beach shack, tucked away from the bustling crowds. The place had a rustic charm, with wooden tables set on the soft sand, fairy lights twinkling above. A live band played the songs of the '90s in the corner, their soft, soulful music blending perfectly with the sound of crashing waves. The nostalgic tunes made the atmosphere feel even more magical.

Sana glanced at the menu, then at Ajay, remembering that he was a vegetarian and usually stayed away from alcohol. Hesitantly, she asked, "Should we order some nice mocktails?"

Ajay looked at her for a moment before a playful smile curved his lips. "Sana, let's order beer."

She raised an eyebrow, surprised. "Beer? But you don't drink."

He chuckled, leaning in slightly. "I do, occasionally... especially when I'm out with colleagues. Sometimes, it's hard to avoid."

Sana smiled, feeling a strange warmth in her heart. It was these little things—his surprises, his willingness to let loose with her—that made their time together even more special. They placed their order, and soon, the chilled mugs of golden draught beer arrived. The frothy liquid glistened under the soft shack lights, and as Ajay took his first sip, he let out a satisfied sigh.

Sana giggled, watching him. "Looks like someone is enjoying the moment."

Ajay reached for her hand across the table, his fingers tracing slow, lazy circles on her skin. "How can I not? I'm with you."

He looked at her for a long second before speaking again.

"Sana, I know I couldn't give you much back then—not the comfort, not the courage you needed," Ajay said, gently holding her hand. "But now, away from everything, all I want is to spoil you with the love and luxury you always deserved."

Sana looked into his eyes, her heart melting at his words. A soft smile curved on her lips.

"And yet, all I ever needed was you," she whispered, brushing her fingers along his knuckles.

She leaned forward, resting her head lightly on his shoulder. The cool night air carried the scent of beer and the salty ocean, creating a relaxed and dreamy atmosphere.

As they sipped their drinks and exchanged lingering glances, the space between them felt warmer, filled with unspoken emotions and a quiet longing.

Love didn't always need grand declarations—it was in the silences, the soft looks, and the gentle grip of two hands that never wanted to let go.

"In the quiet moments,
love whispers the loudest."

Chapter 21

Living in the Bubble

The next morning, they checked out of the beautiful retreat, their hearts full of cherished memories. But Sana was unusually quiet, lost in thoughts that weighed heavy on her mind. Ajay noticed her silence and couldn't ignore it any longer.

Although the love between them felt undeniable, Sana couldn't shake the questions that lingered in her mind. Their days had been filled with love, and they had grown so close again. But was this all just temporary? There was no label to their relationship. Why was it that he only showed her this affection during trips? Why couldn't he take a stand for them, for what they shared? These thoughts weighed heavily on her heart.

Everything felt so perfect... so why was he holding back from commitment?

And now, a quiet discomfort stirred within her—not because she regretted loving him, but because she feared she was losing herself in a story that still had no ending.

Just before they left, he gently pulled her aside.

"Sana, what's wrong? I've been noticing you since morning. Something is bothering you—please, just say it. I hate playing this guessing game."

Sana took a deep breath. Her voice trembled slightly, but her words were clear.

"Do you see where we are heading? What happens now, when we go back to our real lives? Here, we lived in a bubble, forgetting everything—our responsibilities, the world outside, who we really are. But love alone isn't enough, not in the society we live in. You are a father, and your family will never accept me. They didn't before, and they won't now. I can't keep living like this, holding onto something that has no name, no future. And more than anything, think about Neil. He's just beginning to heal from everything he's been through. How can I be selfish and drag him into this?"

She paused for a moment, looking away, her eyes glistening with unshed tears.

"And another thing..." Her voice dropped, laced with pain. "When you touch me, I feel like I'm using someone else's property. And maybe that's true. I was never your choice, Ajay. I was an option—you never truly chose me in the first place. I feel deceived. Maybe you had the same kind of intimacy with your wife... and now with me. What am I supposed to do with that thought?"

Sana continued, her words slow but firm. "Do you know what it feels like to be loved in private and ignored in reality? To be treated like a secret?"

Ajay's heart sank. The weight of her words hit harder than he expected. He stepped forward, wanting to hold her, but she took a step back.

"I gave everything, Ajay. All of me. And all I ever wanted... was for you to stand up for us."

Silence wrapped around them like a storm before the thunder.

After the security check they headed to the airport lounge.

Sana sat quietly her coffee untouched, eyes distant. The trip had gone well, but her heart felt heavier than ever. Ajay sat beside her, scrolling through his phone, unaware of the storm within her.

She finally spoke, her voice low.

"Ajay, can I ask you something personal?"

He looked up. "Of course."

"What kind of relationship did you share with your wife?"

He paused. "It wasn't love. I was forced into it. My parents thought it was time. I didn't have the courage to say no."

Sana took a breath. "But marriage is one thing. Intimacy is another. If there was no love, how did that happen? Having a child isn't just pressure—it's a choice."

Ajay looked down. "I tried to make it work. She was my wife. I didn't want to hurt anyone."

Her voice wavered. "So when I was gone, you did what was expected. And when I came back, you followed your heart?"

Ajay stayed silent.

"You say you love me, but is love that easy for you? Something you give when convenient?"

He reached out, but she stopped him with a look.

"I'm not blaming you," she said softly. "I'm just trying to understand. You say you had no choice, but men like you—smart, independent—do have choices. You just didn't speak your truth."

Ajay's voice dropped. "I was scared. Of hurting them."

"And me?" she asked quietly. "You didn't think about how deeply you were hurting me?"

She stood, gathering her bag.

"You say you were trapped, Ajay. But what about me? Where do I fit in your story?"

He had no answer.

As she walked away towards the gate, one thought echoed in her mind:

"Did he ever truly love me? Or was I just his escape?"

On the flight back, she pretended to sleep. Ajay kept stealing glances at her, hoping for a sign, a word, anything to hold on to. But Sana remained still—physically present, emotionally distant.

Once they landed, as they walked toward the baggage claim, Sana suddenly stopped.

"Ajay..." she said, her tone composed but edged with resolve. "I just need some time to digest all this. As a woman who's only ever loved one man in her life, I've stayed loyal. To you. To this love. You think I never got chances to be with anyone else? I did. I just... never wanted anyone else."

Her voice cracked slightly.

"But I need time. To figure out where I really stand in your life."

"Sana, I can't let go, not just because the world doesn't approve of us," Ajay's voice cracked, with vulnerability. "Love isn't just about those fleeting moments when everything feels perfect... It's about being there for each other when the world feels like it's falling apart. I know we've been avoiding the harsh truth, living in this bubble, but I don't want to lose you. I can't lose you." His words hung in the air, desperate and filled with the weight of everything unsaid. Ajay took a deep breath.

"Give me time, Sana. I won't force anything, but I will try to make Neil understand, little by little. I don't want to walk away from you. Please... don't give up on us yet."

Sana's heart ached at his words. She wanted to believe him, but fear gnawed at her. Still, she couldn't deny the love in his eyes. She hesitated, then finally nodded.

"Alright, Ajay... I'll step back. But I can't keep living in the shadows forever. If this has a future, you have to make it real."

Ajay gently held her hand, pressing it to his lips.

"I will."

As they sat in the car, heading back home from the airport, an uneasy silence settled between them. Sana finally broke it, her voice soft but firm.

"Ajay, I know you want to try, but we can't ignore the reality of Neil's emotions. No matter how much he grows, that loss is still a part of him. If we force this, he might never forgive you."

"So, what do you want me to do, Sana? Walk away? Pretend that what we have doesn't exist?" Ajay's irritation was evident now.

His throat tightened. He had always known Neil wouldn't take it well, but hearing Sana say it with such certainty made it feel even heavier. She wasn't just worried—she understood it on a medical and emotional level.

"So, you're saying there's no way?" His voice cracked, betraying the emotions he was trying to hold back.

Ajay slowed the car as they neared the city. He hated this—hated that love alone wasn't enough. It was a package of commitments, fulfilling expectations and priortizing your partner and family pressure. But for now, all he could do was promise himself that he would find a way, no matter how long it took.

Ajay reached for Sana's hand, his grip firm yet pleading.

"Neil's birthday is next month. He wants to celebrate with his close friends. Let's not make any big decisions right now... let me handle this step by step. After his birthday, I'll start hinting things to my family. Just... please, stay with me till then. Don't make any harsh decisions." She exhaled slowly, nodding.

"Alright, Ajay. I'll try. But promise me... if things don't work out, you won't keep me hanging in the dark. I don't want to live on false hope."

"I promise. I just need time... for Neil, for my family, for us."

Sana gave him a weak smile, but inside, she wasn't sure if time would truly change anything.

"Some hearts wait, not out of weakness, but hope."

Chapter 22

The Crossroads of the Heart

Sana walked into the house, her mind racing, her emotions tangled like threads she couldn't undo. Her mother, ever intuitive, immediately sensed the shift in her daughter's energy.

"Sana, what's wrong? It's Ajay, isn't it?" her voice was soft, but knowing. She had watched the bond grow between them—deeper, more complicated, yet never fully secure.

Sana nodded, too tired to pretend otherwise. Her mother sighed, sitting beside her.

"I know what's happening," she said, her tone both gentle and grounded. "You've let him in. But deep down, you also know there's no clear future. You've been through enough heartache already. Don't let this become another wound you carry silently."

Her words struck hard—not because they were harsh, but because they echoed truths Sana had been avoiding.

"Maa... I feel I'm being used now," Sana whispered, her eyes welling up. "I'm the one who has always adjusted in this relationship. He hides me from the world—I've never met his friends. It's like I only exist when we're far away from everything. Like I'm his secret joy, but never his reality."

Her mother listened quietly, her fingers gently rubbing Sana's back as she continued. "I feel so bad, Maa. He loves me when we're away on trips, when it's just us. But in public... he's scared to accept me. And I can't keep shrinking like this."

"If Ajay truly wants you," her mother continued, her eyes steady, "if he's ready to stand by you, to commit, to respect the love you've given so fully—we'll support it. But he can't keep playing it safe while you drift in uncertainty. He needs to honor your love, not just accept it when it's convenient."

Sana swallowed hard. The truth hurt, not because she disagreed, but because she didn't. She had hoped for more.

But hope alone wasn't enough anymore. Hope—or false hope—is what kept her falling for him, again and again, even when reality was screaming otherwise.

"He's become my weakness, Maa," she said, her voice cracking. "And I feel like I'm getting trapped deeper into this relationship. I want to breathe... I'm suffocating in this trap."

Despite her rising strength, Ajay remained her soft spot. And that infuriated her. Why was it always her—the one who understood more, adjusted more, gave more?

What if she had only been filling the gaps in his life while he kept his world untouched? Had she been offering him the depth of a life partner while he offered her the convenience of companionship?

A week passed. Sana buried herself in work. Ajay was caught up in Neil's birthday preparations. And between them, silence. A silence that grew like a wall, brick by brick, each day.

One evening, she sat on the floor of her apartment, wrapped in a blanket, knees to chest, her heart quiet. She wasn't crying.

She was feeling—truly feeling—for the first time in weeks.

The love.

The waiting.

The quiet ache of being sidelined.

She thought of Ajay. The man who made her heart ache in the most beautiful and painful ways.

How he had leaned on her. But never really stood up for her.

"Why did I keep showing up for someone who never truly fought for me?" she whispered into the empty room.

There was no answer. Only the clock ticking, like a gentle reminder of all the time she had given.

And then there was Neil—the boy she had tried so hard to connect with, even from a distance. She never wanted to replace his mother. She only wanted to be someone safe. Someone kind. But in his world, she had always been the outsider.

It hit her, then.

Love that asks you to shrink, to wait, to disappear for someone else's comfort—

Is not love.

It is fear, dressed in affection.

She looked around her apartment—her books, her calm, the scent of her coffee. Everything here was hers. Built from strength. Crafted from healing.

Not borrowed.

Not paused for someone else's decisions.

Not dependent on being chosen.

She was already whole. She was already enough.

And for the first time, that truth didn't ache—it felt empowering.

Just then, her phone lit up.

Ajay calling...

She stared at the screen. Her thumb hovered.

Her heart skipped the familiar beat.

But this time, she didn't answer.

Not out of anger.

Not to hurt him.

But because she had no need to explain her worth anymore.

She had found her peace. And he would either honor it—or lose it.

She couldn't sleep that night. Restlessness gripped her, as the memories—both beautiful and painful—flashed before her eyes. She lay in bed, staring at the ceiling fan, its slow, steady whirl echoing the passage of time, whispering back to her everything she had tried to forget.

She remembered the first time Ajay had looked at her—his eyes soft, full of something unspoken but deeply felt. The late-night calls, the way he held her hand like it was something precious, like it meant the world. And those promises—never fully spoken, yet always lingering in the spaces between them, promises that now felt like distant echoes of a love that could never be fully touched. But it was the silences—the long, painful silences—that cut the deepest. What once felt like pauses now felt like walls between them, growing taller with every passing day.

All she had ever wanted was to be seen. To be acknowledged. To know that she wasn't just an afterthought, not just someone to hold in the shadows. She wanted to be chosen—not in fleeting moments or when it was convenient, but in the light of day, with no hesitation. Not as a secret. Not as an option.

"Sometimes, the hardest part isn't letting go, but learning to live without someone who once made you feel whole."

Chapter 23

When Love is Not Enough

Next day...

"Hello Ajay, I'm sorry I was tired yesterday and couldn't take your call. Hope all is well. How was the birthday party?"

Sana's voice was calm. Clear. But Ajay sensed the shift. There was a distance in her tone he had never heard before. It was as if a wall had quietly risen between them, and though he couldn't see it, he could feel its weight pressing down on him. His stomach twisted, a mixture of confusion and unease bubbling within him.

He was silent for a second. She had never ended a day without speaking to him. Never let a moment go by without a word, a text, an update. But now, everything felt different. The warmth that usually laced her words was gone. This cool, almost distant tone was a stranger to him. And for the first time in their relationship, he realized how much he depended on the comfort of her voice.

Before he could respond, she added, "Can we meet in the evening? I need to talk."

"Yes, Sana. Sure," he replied, his voice strained with uncertainty. "I'll pick you up at 8 p.m."

"Yes, Sana. Sure," he replied, his voice strained with uncertainty. "I'll pick you up at 8 p.m."

There was a pause, and then he added, "Is everything fine, Sana? You sound very different."

His words lingered in the air, filled with the concern he could no longer mask.

He hung up, staring at the phone for a moment longer than he should have. Something didn't feel right. A nagging feeling started to grow in his mind, but he tried to push it away. Maybe it was just a phase. Maybe she was just tired or stressed. He wanted to believe in their bond, the one that had always kept them strong. But deep down, he couldn't ignore the feeling that this time, it was different.

On the other side, Sana was already resolved. She had made up her mind. The coldness in her voice wasn't something she could fake. It was real. This was the first time in a long while she wasn't waiting for him to fix things, to make her feel important, to make her feel seen. She didn't need him to explain himself. She had done enough waiting. Enough sacrificing.

Sana's heart had been pulled in so many directions, but now, it was clear. No more half-answers. No more playing along with a love that only existed in shadows. She had learned the hard way that love, when hidden, could only hurt.

The distance between them felt as real as the silence that stretched across their conversations. And for the first time, she wasn't afraid of it.

She had taken the day off from her clinic, needing space to think things through. She wasn't in the mood to interact with anyone; all she wanted was to be alone, to dive deep into her thoughts and reflect on everything that had led her to this moment. It was a huge decision for her, one that would change the course of her life, and she needed the time to process it all.

As the day slowly passed, so did the waves of anxiety that had been crashing inside her. Each hour felt heavy, but with every breath, she found a little more clarity. By the time the clock struck 8 p.m., she was composed—quiet on the outside, but steady within.

Ajay arrived to pick her up, just as he said he would. The familiar sound of his car outside stirred something in her chest, but this time, she didn't rush. She took a final look at herself in the mirror—not to check how she looked, but to remind herself of the strength she now carried.

And then, she stepped out. Ready to face what needed to be said.

Ajay opened the door for her, just like he always did—gentle, thoughtful, like nothing had changed. But everything had.

Sana stepped in slowly, her smile soft but distant. As she settled into the seat, she looked into his eyes—not searching for answers this time, but memorizing them, as if it were the last time she'd see that familiar gaze.

There was a quiet weight in that look. A silent goodbye hiding behind the curve of her lips.

Ajay sensed it too. The warmth he was used to wasn't there. Her presence felt calm, but not comforting—it was composed, like someone who had finally made peace with a decision that hurt.

It was a quiet night as they drove through their favorite place—the expressway.

It was a quiet night as they drove through their favorite place—the expressway.

This place had always been their escape, their secret little world away from the noise and rush of life. Whenever they needed time together, just the two of them, away from the crowd and traffic, they would often come here for long, endless drives.

The road, the breeze, the open sky—everything here had witnessed their stolen smiles, whispered dreams, and moments of unspoken love.

But tonight, the same road felt heavy. The memories hung in the air, bittersweet and haunting.

Everything that had once begun here... now seemed to be slowly coming to an end.

The sky above shimmered with stars, the scent of dew fresh and oddly nostalgic.

This road had once been their escape. A place where the world paused, and their love felt unshaken. That night, *"Humein Tumse Pyaar Kitna..."* played softly. A song that once brought smiles now felt heavier than ever.

They didn't sing along. They sat in silence. Not empty—but full.

Full of all the things they didn't say.

Full of what had been—and what could no longer be.

And then, finally, the silence broke...

"In the end, silence spoke louder than love, breaking a heart built on false hopes."

Chapter 24

Not Every Love Gets a Forever

"I can sense something's wrong, Sana. Your silence... it's killing me."

Ajay's voice cracked slightly, his eyes searching hers, desperate for an answer.

"Did I do something wrong?" he asked, his words filled with confusion.

Sana gave him a sad, almost rueful smile. "You didn't do anything. And maybe that's the problem."

Ajay's gaze sharpened, a flicker of understanding beginning to take root.

"I kept waiting, Ajay," she said, her voice steady but laced with emotion. "

She paused, her heart heavy with everything she had been holding back. "You didn't. And I kept accepting less, telling myself it was enough. That time would fix it."

Her voice softened, but the strength in her words only grew stronger.

"But last night, sitting alone while you celebrated with your son... I realized something. I wasn't sad you didn't ask me to come. I was relieved I chose not to."

"Sana, I wanted to protect you from—"

"From what?" she interrupted, her tone gentle but unwavering. "From your parents' anger? From your guilt? Or from Neil?"

Ajay fell silent. "I wasn't asking you to fix everything," she continued, her voice calm but firm. "I was asking you to choose me with the same clarity I chose you."

Sana turned away slightly, her gaze drifting to the window, her thoughts becoming clearer with each passing second. "I love you, Ajay. I probably always will. But I can't keep loving you halfway. I can't keep waiting for a man who's still undecided while I'm tearing myself apart trying to be enough for everyone."

Ajay's gaze softened, but Sana saw the truth in his eyes now—he was finally seeing what she had been blind to for so long. She wasn't angry.

She wasn't bitter.

She was done.

"I'm not leaving because I'm unloved," she said, her voice quiet yet resolute. "I'm leaving because I've finally started loving myself more."

Her eyes shone with unshed tears, but her voice remained steady. "You'll always have a place in my heart. But not in my future."

Ajay's expression faltered, shock painting his face.

"I gave you everything, Ajay," she said, her voice trembling, but it was the tremor of strength, not weakness. "My heart, my soul, my body. I went against my parents, against society's expectations, and still, I chose you. I loved you with everything I had. I was ready to do whatever made you happy."

She let out a breath, her eyes meeting his with a painful clarity.

"But somewhere along the way, I forgot myself. I lost who I was. I stopped asking what I wanted. I stopped dreaming my own dreams. All I cared about was making sure you were okay, that Neil was okay, that everything around you stayed peaceful."

Her voice cracked slightly, but she didn't break. "I didn't even realize when I became someone who was always waiting—waiting to be accepted, to be seen, to be loved fully. And now... I can't do it anymore, Ajay."

Her tone grew stronger, and she stood taller, resolute in her decision. "I choose myself now. My happiness. My peace. My self-respect. That doesn't mean I don't love you. I do. Maybe I always will. But I can't keep loving you in a way that breaks me."

Sana looked into his eyes, no anger in her gaze, only the raw truth of what she had come to realize. "So please... don't talk about me at your home. Don't try to convince Neil. Don't keep me hanging in between two worlds anymore."

A single tear escaped down her cheek, but her voice remained firm, unshaken. "I'm done holding myself back. I'm not yours to fight for anymore. I'm mine now."

Ajay's lips parted as if to speak, but no words came. He saw it now—she wasn't asking him to stop her. She was already gone.

The weight of her words sank into him like stones, each one heavier than the last. He stood there, helpless, caught in a cage of his own making. His heart ached, not just for losing her, but because he knew, deep down, it was his own failure that had driven her to this point.

It wasn't that he didn't love her. He did, in a way that tore him apart. But he had never found the courage to stand up for her—never found the strength to choose her above the voices that had always controlled his life. First, it was his parents, their expectations suffocating him. And now, it was Neil—the child who was already scarred by loss, and yet another burden Ajay couldn't lift.

As the car pulled away, the silence between them thickened, suffocating the very air around him.

Sana stepped out of the car. The night sky above was clear, the stars shining brightly, but they couldn't compare to the clarity that had settled within her. She stood there for a moment, arms wrapped around herself, gathering all the broken pieces of the past and holding them gently, as if acknowledging them before releasing them.

She looked up at the sky and let a soft, bittersweet smile touch her lips—as if seeking strength from the stars, silently asking God to help her gather the courage to walk away, to unlove the man she had once dreamed of forever with. Her heart trembled, aching to cry out, to ask Ajay *why he never chose her loud enough, proud enough, whole enough.* But she swallowed the storm inside. Because some endings deserve grace, not noise.

The silence between them wasn't just a pause—it was an answer.

Ajay's voice cracked as he said her name, but even as the words left his lips, he knew she was right. She wasn't asking for anything now. She wasn't waiting anymore.

Sana quietly sat in the car and Ajay joined her silently.

As the car drove away, a suffocating silence filled the space between them. The world outside was distant, but inside, their hearts echoed with the fading remnants of what they once had. Ajay thought of all the stolen moments, the promises left unsaid, and the future that had never truly belonged to them.

Sana, too, was lost in her own thoughts. She thought of the sacrifices, the compromises, the endless waiting. But through all of it, she stayed strong. Because she knew, deep in her heart, that this was the right decision.

Maybe this was the last time he would drop her off, the last time she would look at him with hope. So many unspoken promises, so many opportunities lost to fear. A future they once painted in whispers had slowly crumbled under the weight of his silence, his hesitations.

But she was done waiting. She stepped out quietly, closing the door behind her. That soft click was the sound of an end, the end of something once thought unbreakable.

A deep, aching silence filled the car—no longer just in the car, but in their hearts.

>A silence that didn't scream but echoed.
>
>And in that stillness, they both knew—
>
>Because Love wasn't always enough.

"True strength isn't in holding on; it's in knowing when to let go, not out of anger, but out of self-respect."

Epilogue

Seasons changed. Time, relentless and unyielding, moved forward, as it always does.

Life didn't wait for heartbreak to heal.

But Sana had found her rhythm again. Quiet mornings with coffee in hand, long days at the hospital, and peaceful nights in her little sanctuary, where books, music, and calm ruled.

There were moments when Ajay's name would flicker in her thoughts—a song, a familiar place, a laughter that echoed in the air. He had been her first true love—raw, intense, unforgettable. She didn't deny it.

But love, she had learned, could never come at the cost of losing yourself.

She smiled when his memory crept up, and sometimes, tears came too. But no longer were they tears of regret. They were soft, gentle reminders of how deeply she had loved and how bravely she had let go.

She hadn't shattered.

She had bloomed.

Not because she didn't love him anymore—but because she had learned to love herself more.

Now, Sana stood strong in her career. Patients admired her. Her juniors looked up to her. Her name carried weight. The dreams she once buried beneath compromises now stood tall beside her, visible, respected. She walked through life with grace—a grace forged from pain, yet rebuilt through self-respect.

Across the city, Ajay sat one evening, flipping through old photographs. A faint, bittersweet smile lingered on his lips, his heart heavy with the weight of what had been lost. He hadn't just lost a woman. He had lost a love—patient, powerful, pure—that he hadn't known how to protect.

He often wondered what might have been... if he had been braver, if he had given her the love she deserved.

Neil, now grown, had shed his confusion and grief. He understood life better now, and with time, the anger that had once defined him began to fade.

One day, as he spoke to a friend, he said, quietly but with depth,

"Sana wasn't just someone who loved my dad... she helped him live again. And maybe, in some way, she helped me too."

Ajay, overhearing, felt the sting of those words. His eyes burned with unshed tears.

Maybe, someday, life would bring them face to face again—on a crowded street, in a bookstore, at an airport. Perhaps they would share a smile.

Or maybe, just a quiet nod.

But for now... Sana had already written her ending.

Not as the woman left behind.

But as the woman who chose herself.

With love. With courage. With grace.

That evening, standing by her window, the sky painted with shades of gold and lilac, she closed her eyes, her hand resting gently on her heart.

"I chose myself," she whispered to the night.

And that... was enough.

Behind the Scenes: From My Heart to Yours

Every book carries a hidden journey — not just the journey of the characters, but also the journey of the writer. When I first thought of Sana and Ajay, I didn't know their love would break my own heart as I wrote it. I had imagined a love story full of passion, a fairy tale. But the truth is, love is not always what we see in movies or read in fairy tales.

Why I wrote this book?

This story was born from my desire to explore the delicate balance between love and self-respect. In love, one becomes vulnerable and weak, but that doesn't mean love should make you lose yourself. Some people stay in toxic relationships out of fear of abandonment, but the truth is, choosing yourself is the first step toward self-love. I wanted to write about love that isn't perfect, love that teaches us the importance of valuing ourselves and recognizing our worth. Love deeply and invest in it — but only if you are valued and treated with respect. Never allow yourself to be just an option to anyone. This story reflects that powerful choice to love oneself, even when it's painful, and to move forward, stronger than befor.

Ajay's Character:

Ajay's character, for me, was real — someone who loved deeply but was always aware of his responsibilities. The weight of his family's expectations, his need to do what was right for them, made him choose a path that led him to let go of the woman he loved. He loved her, yes, but he could never commit. He was never able to take a stand for his love, and in doing so, he kept her clinging to false hope — a hope that he would never truly fulfill.

Sana's character:

Sana was like a garden, blooming with love and hope, she believed in love, dreaming of fairy tales where love conquers all. She longed to be loved for who she was. Despite Ajay's failure to commit, she loved him deeply. But when he couldn't take a stand for their love, she chose to walk away and choose herself, knowing that love alone wasn't enough.

Why I chose this ending?

I could have written a perfect love story where they found each other, got married and lived happily ever after. But I chose not to, because life isn't defined by idealized dreams or perfect endings. It's shaped by the messy, real moments that love brings — full of growth, heartache, and tough choices. Sometimes, the truest love stories are the ones that don't end perfectly, but rather, teach us about letting go, choosing ourselves, and finding peace in the journey.

www.ingramcontent.com/pod-product-compliance
Lightning Source LLC
LaVergne TN
LVHW041843070526
838199LV00045BA/1408